Wild Wood

'And so a gallant band was formed, to bring about
the downfall of the rich uncaring few. They were the
Wild Wood Volunteers, and theirs is a saga of
poverty and desperation, loyalty and treachery,
strange love and great despair.'

*From the notes of Cedric Willoughby,
Chronicler and Historian*

D1514381

For Viv

And for Matti and Wilf

Wild Wood

JAN NEEDLE

ILLUSTRATED BY
WILLIE RUSHTON

GOLDEN
DUCK

Published 2014 by Golden Duck (UK) Ltd
Sokens, Green Street,
Pleshey, nr Chelmsford,
Essex CM3 1HT
www.golden-duck.co.uk

First published by André Deutsch

ISBN 978-1-899262-21-2

Designed by Matti Gardner and Kate Fox

Printed and bound in the UK by
Biddles Books Limited, King's Lynn, Norfolk

Contents

TROUBLE BREWING — 1

BEAST AND THE BEAUTY — 7

WHOLE LOT OF LIQUOR — 11

THE PROPHET OF DOOM — 18

MAKING THE WELKIN RING — 30

BAXTER MEETS HIS MADMAN — 41

A CHIVVYING UP — 56

INSULT TO INJURY — 67

A STORMY MEETING — 75

DOLLY IN TEARS — 92

'PUT MONEY IN THY SOCK' — 103

LIGHTNING STRIKES TWICE — 115

'VOLUNTEERS WILL WIN THE DAY' — 124

THE ARREST — 136

LOVELY WEATHER FOR AN INVASION — 145

DOLLY DROPS A BOMBSHELL — 158

O.B. STOPS THE ROT — 166

BAXTER'S FLYING COLUMN — 178

THE CHASE — 191

'TIS DARK AND LURKS THE NAUGHTY DEED' — 200

GOODBYE DOLLY — 210

EPILOGUE: 'THE MAD OLD GENTLEMAN' — 215

APPENDICES — 223

WILD WOOD was first published in 1981, with original illustrations by the late great satirist Willie Rushton. Willie's son Toby was in on the earliest discussion of the pictures – he and his father were dressed in tennis whites and enacting Wimbledon on the table tennis table in their living room the day Jan Needle met them – and thanks are due both to Toby and to André Deutsch for permission to base this edition on the much-loved original.

Rapidly a cult bestseller, Wild Wood was broadcast on BBC Radio 4, and has been variously dramatised. It has been translated into several languages, including Japanese.

Intended for both adults and children, it numbers among its admirers former deputy Labour party leader Roy Hattersley (Mail on Sunday), Joanna Carey of the Guardian ('a brilliant retelling'), academic critic Ann Wright ('Truly comic descriptions of political realities'), and writer and critic Jan Mark ('I honestly wish I had written this book').

Jan Needle lives in the North of England, and has written more than forty books, as well as TV, stage plays, animations and radio. His novels include thrillers, historical sea books, criticism, humour and contemporary fiction. Many of them are also available as E-books on Amazon. He has five children, five boats, and even more musical instruments.

How it all began

Chapter One
TROUBLE BREWING

There's been so much stuff and garbage talked about the 'time of troubles' down the years, that I think the actual facts should see the light of day at last. I'm only a common or garden nobody name of Baxter, maybe, but the mad old gent who ran me over at the crossroads, for instance, said it was bigger than the Peasants' Revolt, whatever that was. He was a journalist so shouldn't be believed, that's obvious – but who's he calling peasants, eh? It's a blind disgrace.

Fact of the matter is, that tales of mayhem, articles in the papers, even the odd book or two, has done us not a bit of good at all. It's made folks look down their noses on us, more than they even did before, it's made us into criminals and ne'er-do-wells.

Even worse, while the Wood's been painted as a sink hole full of scroungers and low-life, the ones who started it, the ones who'd still be locked in prison if they weren't so blessed rich, got off scot-free. Oh, there's two sides to every story, let me tell you – and our side ain't even never seen the light of day.

Not that I'm complaining, like, because I'm not that sort of feller, when it comes to it. I'm a Wild Wooder born and bred, and my ma, gawd bless her cotton socks, brung me up to make the best of what was flung at me, good or bad. And truth to tell, I think she's right. It was a wild time, fair enough. A rough time and a riotous, that cost me some friends and the young female I loved above all others in the world. But it was the best of times an'all, like the man once said. The best times and the worst.

We're rough down in the Wild Wood, and my talk's a wee bit makeshift, but to try and help you understand, I'll tell a thing they used to say about us, like a sort of joke, or riddle. No one can remember who said it first, but it caught on quick, and became a kind of proverb: '*A weasel's easily distinguished, ferret's stoatily different.*'

Well it gets a laugh all right, but it's true an'all, a hundred and ten per cent as they say nowadays. Which sounds a lot, but no more than the difference between chalk and cheese, eh? We're different, whatever anyone outside might think. And it's the differences that matter in this story.

Another thing that tends to get overlooked, is that back at the turn of the last century, when all this happened, things wasn't quite like they are today. I'm old now – ancient even – but I can remember them times. My grandad didn't get a pension like I do. And when there was a real cruel winter, like there was in '06 and '07, there was no Meals on Wheels for the old 'uns or government hand-outs for them with families. When times was hard and the Soup Kitchen didn't turn up, we went hungry. Bread and dripping was a luxury sometimes, I can tell you.

Anyway, looking back on it, I reckon it was them two hard winters, coupled with a mite of bad feeling that had been growing up for some time over the goings on of a certain well-known individual and his friends, that led to the blow-up. The thing was, when times were cruel and appeared to be getting worse, the few animals that were well provided for stood out starker. There wasn't many, true enough; and there was a lot of us. That only seemed to make it worse.

I was very young at the time, but I was big for my age and as bright as a button. My old man had passed on some years before, so I'd had to work from pretty early on to help eke out the money. The farmer who'd gave me a start was a modern-minded chap for them days, and went in for machinery,which he let me tinker with, as much as I liked. It didn't do much good in terms of advancement, but it gave me something not many other animals had. I had knowledge. I could take down and rebuild engines and machinery. I could do steam, farm gear, and the even more new-fangled stuff; the type of vehicle that my old mother called 'infernal combustion'. What's more, I could drive.

This was because the gaffer was what used to be called a 'gentleman farmer'. He didn't do it because he needed the money, but because he wanted to. He liked the noise of sheep baaing, he liked to see the rosy-cheeked country girls milking the cows, and he liked to breed great muscular horses to pull the waggons about. He liked motor vehicles, too, which was funny in a way, because most of the farmers who'd even heard of them saw them at the very best as new-fangled contraptions designed to make lazy animals lazier, which would no doubt be a nine-days wonder before they faded from memory along with other silly inventions, like the phonograph, say, or the aeroplane. But although he liked the new things, the gaffer wasn't the sort to get his hands dirty. When he bought his first petrol wagon, and the men that delivered it had left, he called me over to lift the bonnet open for him.

We stood there looking in. It was a rare and lovely sight, let me tell you. She was a Throgmorton Squeezer, with coil ignition and hand-polished journals. Six cylinders, each big enough to brew cider in. And powerful! She could carry four ton, and would have made near thirty miles an hour, given her head. God help the fellow walking in front with the red flag, though!

In them days, of course, they built them different. None of your mass produced cast-iron blocks with a die-cast serial number. The engine was all gleaming brass tubes and finger knobs. There was a little face carved on the bleeder nipple, and the fan blades were painted different colours so as they made a pattern when you revved the engine.

The gaffer stared in for a while, and I positively drooled.

'Well, young feller,' he said. 'Think you could drive her, then?'

I didn't realise for a while that he meant me. When it sunk in I rubbed my eyes and jumped up and down. Cut quite a caper. Until he said: 'Well if you *don't* think—' And I leapt in the cab as though I'd been shot.

'Drive it?' I says – for I was a cocky young fellow enough, and quite willing to have a crack at absolutely anything once, not to mention most things twice and some things more times than was good for my health – 'Why, I'll drive it, your honour. Where do you want to go?'

'Forty Acre field,' he said. Very wise too, for it was wide, flat and empty.

So I advanced the ignition, wiggled the toggle springs – wound the handle. Retarded the ignition, jiggled the priming sleeve – wound the handle. Lifted the bonnet, scowled at the little grinning face on the bleeder nipple, thought better of it and chucked it under the chin – wound the handle. Billy Bingo! She caught with a hiss and a roar. The whole Throgmorton jounced and shook on its bright yellow, solid-tyred, wooden-spoked wheels.

The gaffer gave a great shout of 'Come on, Baxter, damn you!' and I leapt into the cab and seized the gear stick. I was blind with excitement and drunk with power. I pressed a pedal here, pushed the lever forward with total confidence, pulled a handle there, pressed a knob there and threw a switch here. The truck howled in a loud and rather anguished way, rose several inches into the air, settled back on its springs – and raced off. How we bounced and shouted! I pushed and pulled at the wheel, banged at the pedals with both feet, crashed the gears. When we reached Forty Acre I shot round and round, Gaffer grabbed the klaxon, and we chased and terrorised everything in sight. We was transported!

One way and another it was quite a costly do. Three hens took the unusual step of flying away and finding a quieter farm, one of the older milkmaids came all over queer and had to be pensioned off into her own tied cottage, and all but three of the cows refused to give milk for six days. But as the farmer said when we ran out of petrol at long last, and came to an eerie and silent stop among the settling dust: It was worth it. It was *well* worth it.

Of course, the differ between being rich and being poor is a big one. After that one first mad fling, sobriety had to come. For despite the fact he'd been with me, I'd forgotten myself quite enough for a long, long time to come, and no mistake. Gaffer never referred to the incident again, and neither did anyone else. But I did notice sixpence had been docked from my pay that Friday, and I didn't need it spelling out that it was for the time I was gadding about in the old Squeezer. I'm only grateful he didn't see fit to charge me for the petrol, as some would have done in them good old days.

But it did teach me something that meant quite a lot in view of events that started later that year or early the next. I'm not saying I'm better than anyone else, and I'll admit that I got a mite carried away one way and another over motor vehicles. But I reckon that was the single time in my whole long experience that I actually did anything that could have been condemned by anyone. And as I've said, Gaffer was with me, and he was an accessory before, during and after the fact.

Chapter Two
BEAST AND THE BEAUTY

My fault or not, though, the lesson had been learned, not just by me but by the farmer, too. I don't how much that waggon might've cost – I can't begin to dare to imagine – but the Throgmorton Squeezer was a big beast, and main hard to handle. But she was designed to work and so, as I had been brought up to believe, was I. So I settled down to learn how to handle her, before he changed his mind and sent me down the road.

First I had to get the hang of just looking after the thing. Every day I got to the farm at half past five, after a breakfast of a cup of tea and porridge with a slice of Mother's bread. At this time we was quite well off, although there were six other children besides me, so I was usually able to have a smudge of jam with it. When I got there, I was meant to begin by checking the animals in my charge, but more and more this went to someone else while I tended the machines. Naturally, it was a case of starting from scratch. Every inch of the Throgmorton had to be polished till it gleamed. Of course, it was hand-painted and every inch a beauty, so it was no labour. Under the bonnet, likewise. Well, I've told you about the brasswork. I used to rub away until my arm near broke. That little face I mentioned positively smiled at me. And from the first time till the last, I used to chuck it under the chin before I swung the starting handle. Never failed. A pity that some other people never learn how to treat a motor vehicle; the world would be a pleasanter place.

After the polishing came the checks. Farm work's dusty, naturally. So the air filters needed a daily clean, the oil filter had to be changed once a week, and the oil itself needed a careful looking-at morning and night for traces of dirt, metal shavings, or water. Fan belts to tension, mountings to run a spanner over, radiator to top up. Three quarters of an hour every single morning, Sundays included, in the freezing barn with a hurricane lantern. I used to bless me old mother for that hot strong tea and crusty bread.

Unfortunately I couldn't devote all my time to the Squeezer. I had to give a hand to old Tetley, the chap in charge of the traction engines, for a start. He was getting on a bit, and wasn't so hot at humping coal any more. I used to like steam work, but I'd sort of outgrown it when the petrol-jobs came along.

It was such a tedious business. Old Betsy, the biggest engine, took what seemed ages to get up a head of steam. Then for all her glowing, hissing and clanking, she could only make five or six miles an hour, and got bogged down if you took her off the path onto a softish field. Nowadays people hanker after steam, and it's not surprising, looking at the apologies for cars you see flying around, but shifting several hundredweight of coal every morning, rain or shine, hail or snow; well, when the petrol came along it was like a new dawning, for me at any rate.

So. By nine o'clock I was generally clear, unless one of the ploughs, or the harrows, or the seeders or some other piece of boring implementary needed smithing. I could go back to the Squeezer's barn and get her out. This was the big moment. I'll say this for Gaffer, when he got something new and interesting he didn't rush at it like a bull at a gate. He wanted me to learn about that vehicle, and he wanted me to learn proper. At first he used to get the spare hands to push the truck into the open. Except when it was raining, when he'd not allow her to see the light of day at all, for a while. So I'd reach up and open the door, climb into the cab with one foot on the front mudguard, then slide sideways into the seat. Every time I sat there I felt grand; that big leather seat was like a throne. It was off with the handbrake, check that my wings were clear, and a rousing shout of 'Righto, boys! Start shoving!' The Throgmorton Squeezer would roll silently and sedately into the wintry sunshine and stand there gleaming.

Master often climbed into the passenger side then, to sit and watch while I checked the controls and got the hang of everything. It was a complicated business, I can tell you; not just a case of putting in a key and turning it till the thing started. There was a funny old choke lever, all pulleys and wire, the ignition spark timer, that slid up and down the column, and a lot more besides. You really needed three hands, all in all. But it was possible to drive the lorry with only two. Just.

It was three weeks after our mad high-jink in the Forty Acre that the gaffer let me start her up again. I went pale with the responsibility, and said: 'Do you think I'm ready yet, master? She's a big one to handle, and no mistake.'

'No mistake is the word, Baxter,' he said. 'This here waggon cost me hundreds and hundreds of pound. One scratch and I'll have your tail off.'

I swallowed, although my mouth was as dry as a moth's wing. He may just have not been joking, seeing as how things were around about this time.

Well, to cut down a long story, I hopped out, trying to put a brave face on it, chucked the little chin, wiggled this and woggled that, and swung the handle. *Broom!* Off first time. I put it ever so gently into gear and inched forward. Oh my, but we *was* being serious and high-minded! The master looked straight ahead and said not a word, and I behaved the same. We trundled across the yard like a funeral carriage, and when Cecilia, the deaf old goose, looked as though she'd walk in front of us, I didn't even *reach* for the klaxon. I drew up, applied the handbrake, stepped down, and helped her out of the path. Back into my nice warm seat, twice round the main buildings, and back to the barn. I felt as if I'd been to the South Pole single-handed!

But the gaffer was very pleased. 'Baxter,' he said, 'you've done exceedingly well, boy. You shall finish half an hour early tonight.'

And so I left the farmyard to trudge the half-mile to the family hole at only a quarter past eight.

Chapter Three
WHOLE LOT OF LIQUOR

For the past couple of days my mother had been malting barley for her annual autumn brewing session. Vast sacks of the grain had gone through the long, messy and aromatic process. The oven had been on day and night, and my younger sisters and brothers had worked themselves into whimpering and exhausted heaps from scouring the nearby undergrowth for suitable wood for faggot-making. I often wished, when I'd been one of the faggot-makers, that Mother had either never been given the secret of brewing, or we could afford to go to the maltsters for our annual supply of germinated and roasted barley, like better-off animals. However, now I was of beer-drinking age I was extremely glad that she scorned such short cuts. For Daisy's Special, as her bitter beer was known throughout the Wood, was enough to grow hairs on a frog; and most of it found its way down my own long and thirsty neck!

When I got home, she looked up sharply.

'What are you doing back so early, you young rogue?' she asked. 'Not got the sack, have you?'

I savoured the breath of hops that leaked from a huge bubbling iron pot on the fire.

'Not likely, old girl,' I said, impudent-like, but full of myself as you know. 'Got an early cut from Gaffer. On account of a good day's work on the Squeezer.'

'The Squeezer? The Squeezer? What are you talking about?' she said irritably. 'And don't you be so saucy, neither. Not too big to take a clout with me ladle, young fellow, so bear it in mind.'

She was tied up in her brewing, though, and not that interested in my triumph, so I left it be.

'Finished the malting then, Mother?' I asked. 'For them's hops I can smell a'bubbling, isn't them? Making some old vinegar, are you?'

She aimed a friendly clout at me – which being as how I was expecting I dodged easy enough – with the ladle. The kids all fell around, squeaking and laughing. 'Vinegar indeed! You're as cheeky as a weasel,' she said. 'Get on with you and find your supper. Dolly,' (this to my eldest sister) 'get Baxter some bread and cheese and a morsel of that gingerbread.'

Dolly was inclined to argue.

'But Ma, I'm watching the brewing. How will I ever learn to brew like you if you keep sending me out on fool's errands? I'll forget it all again!'

She didn't get anywhere on this line, of course. The big iron ladle changed tack and whistled through the air. Dolly wasn't so sharp as she might have been, and it caught her a smart clap just where her bustle would have been if she'd been a lady. She let out a whoop and shot off, while the little'uns fell about a lot more. The noise was terrific.

'That Dolly,' said Mother. 'She's worse than you are, Baxter. Third year running she'd been watching the brewing, and she hasn't a ghost of a notion. I let her try her hand at the last of the malting today, so we'll be three gallons down on last year. It's not fit to choke a pig on.'

Brewing in our particular ferret hole was a really incredible business. As I sat and chewed my bread and cheese, the first five gallon batch of malt and hops was ready to come off the fire. Three of the youngest lads – Chalmers, Bigsy and Jones – had been cutting and softening the corks and washing out the stone bottles. These now came clattering and chinking in, in huge rush baskets. My mother, meanwhile, aided by Dolly, the smaller but less hamfisted Lucy, and Saunders, a brother, was hoisting the bubbling cauldron off the fire with a chain and two great wooden-handled hooks. Suddenly they upended it and sent the contents whooshing into a vast stone vat that held an amazing number of gallons. The stone was cold, the wort was boiling, and the steam was horrendous. The whole low-ceilinged kitchen disappeared in a hot swirling hop-flavoured mist, to the delight of the shrieking childer.

Of course, they'd got it all wrong and started a row.

'What are you doing, you silly young ferrets?' howled my mother. She'd stepped on a stone bottle, sent it flying, broken two more, and knocked a dish of butter over. The young ones ran about shrieking as she laid around her with a handy wooden spoon. 'We don't need bottles yet, you daft little creatures! It ain't even fermented yet! Oh, heaven smile at me to be blessed with such a brood!'

Two more bottles and a plate were broken in the chase, which everyone enjoyed immensely, then the little ones were packed roaring off to bed, helped by the biggest. Mother and I quietly filled the cauldron with water again, and added the necessary malt, along with a carefully weighed muslin bag of best Kent Fuggles hops. We got the fire up to its hottest under the vessel, noted the time it started to boil on the big old railway clock, and sat down with a sigh at the deal table. This was the moment I had been waiting for.

'Well,' she said at last. 'Do you think you could manage to get a couple of Brewdays up from the cellar without dropping at least one of them?'

Now 'Brewday' was one of Daisy Ferret's wonders, and a great tradition to boot. Made from peculiar quantities of best malt and hops to a recipe of total secrecy – Mother alone knew it, having formulated it herself – it was of the barley wine type; indeed it was undoubtedly the king of all barley wines.

When my father had been alive, a small barrel of it was kept in a dark and forbidden corner of the cellar, for winter use only. When the nights closed in and the air began to get raw, the thought of that barrel used to steal into his mind at the least appropriate moments. He often lost the thread of simple chats about the weather, for instance. For weather chats usually meant people were complaining. Complaints about the weather usually meant it was getting colder. And that meant winter was coming. Winter, to my father, meant Daisy's barley wine. Therefore, I'm afraid, he awaited the onset of the first cold snap with quite indecent impatience.

Come the great day, and everyone in the hole knew it from the moment of waking. He was irritable, impatient, and extremely casual – in a way that anyone could see through. He would drag over his breakfast, insist on a second cup of tea, have trouble finding his overcoat and winter boots (although he'd worn them yesterday) and go off to work with very bad grace indeed.

On his return he would be a strange mixture. Cold, angry at the late hours he had to put in at the farm, hungry and tired. But with sudden and peculiar flashes of jollity, when he'd leap up from his tea and dance a few steps around the kitchen, before sitting down rather sheepish, and snapping at one of us childer for something we hadn't even dreamed of doing! Then every so often his conversation would tail off, and his eyes, if you followed them, would be glued to the cellar door.

Mother always pretended not to know what was in the air. And when he finally wondered, always in the most casual and forced-jovial way, if she didn't think a nip of barley wine might not be a bad thing on such a raw night, she'd reply: 'Barley wine, man! Are you addled? Why, it's not even winter yet. Get off with you!' and bustle about the range, pretending to clean it, or cook something.

Then would start a long and exciting game of wheedling, hectoring and bribery until my father, flushed and triumphant, would be standing expansively with his back to the range, his legs wide apart and a half-pint of the precious brew in his special barley wine mug (for normally, he drank his beer in pints). He would then tantalise himself for what seemed an age, in smelling, noting the colour, admiring the creamy foam, and muttering endearments to the pot. The tension was unbearable, and I always let out a little squeak of excitement when he at last dipped his long pointed nose, took a mouthful, and lifted his head again, the whiskers dripping and foamy, to roll it around his mouth and savour the rich, dark powerful flavour.

The next part was the nicest of all, because we all joined in, in a way. Father would become almost delirious with pleasure and go into raptures of praise for the ale, for his home, for his children, and most of all for his dear wife Daisy: cook, housekeeper, washer of bottles, pickler of pickles, raiser of young.

And brewer.

Then he would drain his first mug in one draught, and dance round the kitchen while we all cheered and sang and beat time with spoons, ladles, fists and feet. It was always a fine start to a loud and lovely evening.

I must report, however, that the next morning was not always so much fun. A small ferret soon learned to keep out of the way of a large one on the morning after a very cold night. All the best things have their dark side.

The barley wine only became Brewday after my father died. Mother decided that the ritual of the barrel was not one she wanted to see maintained among her bright-eyed sons. Apart from anything else, the rather peculiar desire for winter to come early was one she wanted to fade away as part of growing up. Children might like winter, with its snowplay and sledging, but for grown-ups it was a time of hardship and anxiety. Food was scarce, fuel was hard to come by, work was difficult to find and to keep. A bad winter, that started early and finished late, was something to be greatly feared. Items like her barley wine were good in that they helped one forget some of the worst bits – and possibilities – but had to be treated with great caution. The hard facts had to be remembered and faced; in all their starkness and without blurred edges. So the barrel was cleaned and sweetened, and stored in an airy, dry corner. The barley wine henceforward was bottled in nip-sized bottles of about three to the pint.

As it was the last beer she made at her autumn brewing session, she ruled that each batch should not be opened or touched until one year had passed. In fact, that it should be reserved for the few days of actual brewing. Not preparing days, or malting days, but brewdays.

Thus the sweetish, flattish, heavyish, yeasty and beautiful brew was always exactly a year old when it was opened. And a year after my mother's *last* brew, I uncorked and drank the whole posthumous batch, for old times sake, with a few valued friends. A fitting memorial.

Chapter Four
THE PROPHET OF DOOM

Of course, like most well-laid plans, my mother's attempt to push her barley wine into the background did not entirely work out as she had wanted. True enough, she did achieve a much tighter control over it, and she did succeed in making everyone aware of just what dynamite the little stone bottles contained. But the very air of secrecy, the very caution with which the 'Brewday' was in future to be handled, invested it with a new mystique. In short, against her express intentions, a new tradition was born.

So when we sat down in the steamy, aromatic kitchen on that autumn night for a peaceful and ceremonial glass of Brewday apiece, we did not remain alone for long. I had carried up two bottles and drawn the corks while Mother lifted down a couple of thick china mugs. She poured out the tarry black liquor, and we watched each other in silence over the fizzing heads. When they died down a little we raised our pots and sipped together. It was a solemn moment.

The powerful, nutty ale lay heavy on the tongue until the fumes began to rise with the natural heat of the mouth. A fierce, biting flavour caught at the cheeks and begged you to swallow; you couldn't help yourself. Then a hot feeling started in the belly and began to spread upwards, downwards, and outwards. It was like magic. Like swallowing a smooth, gentle fire.

'Billy Bingo, Mother!' I said. 'You've brewed a fair drop of vinegar this time, and no mistake.'

'Better get up another few bottles then, Baxter,' she replied. 'For if I'm not mistaken, I hear footsteps. We've got company.'

It was amazing. For as long as I can remember, there'd be visitors before you'd got halfway down the first mug. Like clockwork they'd be, as though some secret magnet had been switched on with the pulling of the corks, which gripped them by the belt-buckles and hauled them slowly and inexorably through the Wood to the door of our hole. We could have gone for weeks without seeing some of them, or indeed anybody, except in the way of meetings on the woodland paths. But on the first night of brewing we became the centre of attraction.

Mother always seemed a little surprised and flustered by it, but from the magical way a baking of thick gingerbread, not to mention sweet biscuits and spiced buns appeared, it was obvious that she'd actually been expecting it all along – and

19

cooking special, too. For it was the way in them days, that even if you had little for yourselves to eat most of the time, when visitors called, or there was a 'do', you went the whole hog. And a very good custom it was.

Any road, here we were, sure enough, with three enormous clouts on the old door, and a great cry of 'Hello the house! Is there any ferrets within?'

'Dearie me,' said Mother. 'Now whoever can that be? Open the door, Baxter, don't stand about like a clump!'

Ignoring the hard words, which weren't meant anyway, I opened up the door. This year it was the aged ones first. A hoary old stoat called Sherwood, so wrapped up in an old Army blanket-coat that you could only recognise him by his funny eye, another old geezer called Adnam Stoat, and a seafaring rat called Wilson who'd swallowed the anchor and set up as a tobacconist and grocer in the Wild Wood. A strange old fellow, lean and rangy, with a fund of marvellous stories and tales. Doubtful if more than a millionth of them was true, looking back on it, but he got on like a house on fire with everyone, especially the kids. He used to tell stories while measuring out an ounce of jelly beans or Pontefract cakes, and sometimes it would be a quarter of an hour before the screw of paper – always over-full – would be handed across to the bright-eyed and mesmerised young animal on the other side of the counter. Wilson often forgot to take their money, too, even when reminded.

'Well well,' said Daisy, my ma. 'Well well, and this *is* a surprise! Come in, gentlemen, come in and welcome. Baxter!' (This to me, with a vague clout in the general direction of my left ear.) 'Baxter, don't dither, you silly ferret. Take the gentlemen's coats. Can I offer you a drink, sirs?' (Imagine their faces had she *not* done so! Imagine hers if they had refused!) 'It just so happens that my eldest and me have opened the first of this year's special. Brewday, you see. Today we'm brewing.'

As cloud upon cloud of dense, hot, hop-laden steam was roaring out through the still-open door, this remark was a shade unnecessary. Soon the whole Wood – those who had forgotten, at any rate – would know, and probably decide to celebrate the fact with a short neighbourly visit. But our first guests played the game, naturally.

'Good Lord, Mrs Ferret,' exclaimed old Adnam, pulling off his huge woolly comforter. 'We'd never have known. Just happened to be passing, so we thought we'd drop in for a brief chat. What a coincidence!'

The others echoed his surprise, frantically hauling off their heavy outdoor clothes before the super-heated kitchen knocked them unconscious. It was a merry sight, so eagerly were their eyes searching for a glimpse of the famous brew.

Their tongues were positively hanging out, but hardly had the ritual been observed, hardly had they got those long, pink, anxious organs satisfactorily submerged in barley wine, hardly had they had time to smack their lips and offer their genuine and heartfelt congratulations and thanks to the beaming brewer, when the knocker banged again, the door was flung wide once more, and the next wave arrived.

Soon the kitchen was bursting at the seams, and the special drawing room was opened. This only happened two or three times a year, and it was always something of a shock to me. It was a dull, heavy room with sombre furniture and a slight smell of damp. But in not liking it, I was in a minority of one, apparently. Some of the lady animals had turned up now, and they oohed and aahed when the room was flung open. They admired the wide and ill-designed fireplace, which threw all the heat straight up the chimney, gingerly tested the dark, hard chairs and lied about how very comfortable they were, and nodded wisely at the pale wash pictures of imposing buildings and great men.

Gradually, the party sorted itself out, so that the fellows were in the kitchen and the wives inhabited the best room. Mother became the queen of the parlour, and I was lord of the tap-room. I call Mother queen because she became unusually expansive as the evening wore on, and poor Dolly, who had been fast asleep from the exertions of trying to remember the rules of brewing, was made to get up and wait on the ladies. A thankless task enough, as the gentler sex had wrinkled their delicate noses after one tiny tentative taste at the real purpose of the evening, and gone on to insipid country cordials that Mother – a more robust spirit – had made almost contemptuously for young children and finicky females.

Poor Dolly had her work cut out carrying trays of sugar-goodies and jugs of pinky fluid, while I sat grandly in the middle of two piles of nip bottles, which changed in relative size as the number of full ones decreased and of empty grew.

The piles were about equal when an absolutely thunderous hammering nearly took the door from its hinges, and a muffled but enormous roar of 'Hello the house' quietened even the hubbub in the kitchen for a couple of ticks. I let out a great whoop, for I knew at once who it was, having been wondering for ages where they were. Out went the usual vast rush of steam, and in swept my friend O.B. Weasel.

Now O.B. was a flamboyant fellow, even for a weasel, and everybody in the kitchen cheered when he breezed in. He was wearing an incredible checked cape, and big high crowned beaver hat after the style of the clippership captains of the last century. The wild effect was completed by a pair of highly-polished black leather boots that came up well past his knees.

Over his shoulder was slung a stout canvas bag, that doubtless contained one or the other of his fine collection of concertinas. For O.B., among his many other accomplishments, was a noted musician. He came rushing over and flung himself on me, scattering empty bottles all over the kitchen floor.

'Hello Baxter, you old ferret,' he cried. 'Where's the nip that warms, then? Me and my mates are frozen to the bone from trudging the Wild Wood.'

By this time my mother had extricated herself from the parlour, and come to greet the latest arrival. She appeared at the doorway flushed but happy, for it was not many holes that O.B. normally visited, and it was considered something of an honour. She dipped an awkward curtsey, and murmured 'Ah, Mr Weasel. We're honoured, I'm sure.'

O.B. raced across the room, seized her hand, and kissed it resoundingly. Mother blushed a deep red, and got quite flustered.

'Honoured, ma'am?' said O.B. 'Nonsense. The honour is entirely mine. The fame of your special brew is an irresistible attraction, and a great credit to the Wild Wood. I would add that nothing even my illustrious family has ever produced – including myself, their worthless son – has been of half so much merit.'

Mother became an even deeper shade of crimson, but O.B. just kissed her hand again.

'And by the way,' he added. 'Call me O.B., do; and I shall call you Daisy, if I may?'

With poor Mother helpless, it was Dolly, of all ferrets, who came to the rescue. She popped out of the parlour, bright with labour but undaunted, and offered to take his cape. Which she promptly dropped and trod on, in her usual manner. Everybody laughed, even my mother, and the ice was broken.

Coats and hats were chucked onto the pile in the corner, musical instruments were stacked carefully under the table, and the pile of full nips resumed its race to annihilation.

O.B., I should perhaps explain, was held a little in awe by most of the Wild Wooders, because of his family connexions. Although one would never have guessed it from his conduct and mode of dressing, he was the eldest son of the Chief Weasel, and next in line to the position. He was also a brilliant fellow in many respects, knowing foreign languages, and playing on at least three instruments to my certain knowledge. Of course, position among us woodland folk was a relative matter. For all his importance, the Chief Weasel was hardly what you'd call rich. He had a fine extensive burrow and wasn't short of food or drink, but compared with the River Bankers, say, he was financially – and they would no doubt have added socially – decidedly inferior. It was a point which those animals did not tire of making either, unfortunately for friendly relations.

Among us folk such distinctions counted for very little. It was generally accepted that the weasels were the natural leaders, being as they were so bright and inventive, so the Chief Weasel was quite a big noise, one way and another. But that did not stop me from being a great friend of O.B. from an early age, or both of us from getting on very well with some of the younger stoats. We all knew what hard work was (for even O.B. had a job of sorts, as part-time teacher in the little local school) and we all knew what it was to be hungry and cold sometimes.

There was three other animals with O.B. on this occasion, and two of them were also my friends. One was Harrison Ferret, a peculiar, silent chap who was apprentice to the gunsmith in town. He was a sober-sided fellow, old for his age and very absorbed by his work, but he played a good penny whistle, and was an expert fisherman. Then there was another weasel, Radcliffe, who liked eating, drinking and dancing. The dancing was his saving grace, for he had a tendency to fat which his whirling and leaping helped to keep at bay. But my little sister Lucy, who's got a wicked tongue at times, once called him Roly Poly Radcliffe, and it couldn't have been so far out, because it stuck. Unhappily for Roly Poly he liked natty clothes, too, and with his little weasel head, his red and white striped waistcoat, and his shiny black shoes and white spats, he looked a bit like a humming top from a distance.

The last of the party was a stoat, and completely unknown to me, which in itself was odd. He was of medium height but very small in the body, dressed in an austere grey suit of some drab cotton material under his overcoat. His hand knitted scarf was grey, and his head was enclosed in a woollen balaclava that framed his face completely. From the depths of the frame glittered two intensely bright eyes, that seemed to hold anyone they looked at like a hypnotist's. He was extremely thin and hollow-cheeked, with a sombre, serious air that matched the greyness of his clothes. He shook hands with great solemnity, and bowed briefly at my mother. Dolly, I am sad to say, appeared hardly able to take her little pink eyes off him; until Mother, suddenly coming to, caught her a shrewd clout on the side of the head and exclaimed: 'Get off with you, miss! There's ladies to be looked to!'

O.B. lifted his dripping snout from out of an ale jug, and sprayed me with foam from his whiskers.

'Baxter, my boy, that paw you're shaking belongs to a new friend and comrade. Name of Boddington, on account of he's peculiarly yellow, a little lacking in body, extremely bitter, but one of the best!' He laughed uproarious at this, although to this day I've no idea what the joke was; but O.B. was like that. Had a sense of fun and a line in repartee that often left us less worldly animals smiling but baffled. I just said politely, 'Pleased to meet you, Mr Boddington. Make yourself at home. Would you care to try a glass of barley wine? It's Ma's special.'

He smiled a rather frosty little smile.

'Yes, I've heard all about it. But I won't, thanks all the same. I'm not much of a drinker myself.'

I suppose I must have looked startled by this, for in those days a working man who didn't like and appreciate good ale was a rarity. O.B. saw my look and clapped me on the shoulder. 'Don't mind Boddington,' he said. 'He comes from over the river, where they do things different. He may not be a drinking stoat, but you'll get on with him like a house on fire.'

It transpired when we all sat down for a chat that Boddington was related to the biggest stoat family in the Wild Wood, and had recently come across from the next county – the Greenfields – to link up the two branches of the clan. Times on the other side had been very hard, he told us, and a lot of the younger elements had packed their belongings and set out to find better things elsewhere. Even during the summer, jobs had been very scarce, and now winter was clamping down there was a real fear that the food supplies might not stretch for the Greenfielders to see out the winter.

'It's the old, old story,' said O.B., packing his pipe from a vast leather pouch he drew from his waistcoat pocket. 'The grass is always greener on the other side of the valley.'

Boddington tapped out his clay on the side of the fire, and smiled thoughtfully.

'Maybe so, O.B.,' he replied. 'But I didn't count on that. I think times is going to be hard everywhere. The Wild Wood's a good spot, but things ain't getting no easier.'

Harrison chipped in here, in his usual gloomy manner.

'Ah, Boddington's right for sure,' he mumbled. 'Why, even the gentry is feeling the pinch. Orders for shotguns is down considerable this year. Hardly got enough to cover 'is steel order 'asn't the boss. We 'aven't started so many as three special orders for 12-bores in so many months, and as for garden guns... Well, main bad it's been. Boss reckons to go bankrupt if things don't get better soon.'

'Bankrupt?' Boddington gave a little smile that made me feel right chilly. 'You'll be out of a job long before the boss goes bankrupt, man. If orders is down, what's the last thing he needs, eh? People to do a job that don't need doing, that's what. See what I mean, see? Times is bad, and they'll get worse. No talk of grass being greener or nothing. Any grass at all would be welcome, on any side of the valley.'

Roly Poly Radcliffe just told them to stop being so devilish miserable, and enjoy themselves. He had a point, too, tucking in as we all were to sweet gingerbread and smoking the good tobacco that O.B. was dishing out so liberal round the room. But Boddington was not the stoat to be sidetracked. He turned on the gaudily-dressed and overweight weasel.

'It's all very well for you to talk, Radcliffe,' he said. 'Anyone can see that you've never gone short, and it's just a pity that you flaunt your comfortable position so obvious. Things aren't the same for all of us. We live in trying times, and some of us is worried by it.'

Well this floored old Roly Poly, because you had to admit that he had things quite plush, one way and another. He lived on his own in a hole that had been left him by an uncle, and he had enough besides not to have to bother a lot about work. Boddington sensed his victory and pressed his advantage.

'All right, all right,' he said. 'I know I'm fairly new here, but I've got eyes and ears. It's just the same on the other side,

27

you know. Here we all are, poor as church mice, living in cramped, overcrowded conditions without two pennies to bless ourselves with, and there's the other lot and their huge houses, more money than sense, more bedrooms than bodies. It's disgusting.'

He stopped and glared round at us. 'My sisters,' he went on. '*All* my sisters...' He glared round again, pausing dramatically. 'All my *four* sisters – is in service. On the River Bank, every one. And they bring back pennies. Five o'clock in the morning they start, and work till they drop. And they bring back pennies. It's a scandal.'

The argument was beginning to get through, and the kitchen was quieting down considerable. The River Bank always gave us Wild Wooders pause for thought; it was an uncomfortable subject.

It was Wilson the rat who chipped in next. He edged his way up to the fire, pushing aside a couple of us younger ones, and pulling out a burning end of faggot to light up his short, hand-carved seaman's pipe. We all waited until his grey old head was wreathed in a dense cloud of smoke. Wilson was worth a listen. But for once he was not romancing. He puffed quietly for a short while, spat into the glowing embers, and said: 'I'm like young Boddington there myself. A comer-in. A foreigner. An outsider.'

Such was the old rat's popularity, that there was a chorus of denials. But Wilson merely waited till the row had died down, and continued.

'Don't think I don't feel wanted, for I do. But I've not been here as long as most, and I notice things. One thing I've noticed is this.' He suddenly reversed his pipe and jabbed me sharply in the chest with it. 'You, young Baxter. You're a ferret.' He turned to Radcliffe and tapped him lightly on the head. 'Roly

Poly here's a weasel, Boddington's a stoat.' He sipped his ale. 'So we have a ferret, a weasel, and a stoat. But what do we call them? We call them Baxter, Radcliffe, Boddington. There.'

Wilson went back to his pot and his pipe, and a rather puzzled silence descended on the room. He was normally easy to follow, this old yarn-spinner. But we was flummoxed.

For the second time that evening Dolly helped us out; it must have been the cleverest day of her life. It came as a bigger surprise because I didn't know she'd crept in from the parlour to listen. Odder still, she spoke direct to Boddington.

'I think Mr Wilson means the names,' she told him. 'I mean us poor people; there are so many of us, if you know what I mean. I mean, Mr Toad, now. *He* hasn't got a name, has he? Well, if he has I've never heard of it. Just plain Mr Toad.'

The assembled company turned as one man and stared at Dolly. She went pink, then pinker yet. Then she scuttled back into the best room.

In the quiet that followed, Wilson muttered: 'Ah, that's right. Privilege, wouldn't you say, Mr Boddington? Them and us. The teeming masses need a handle to their name like you and me and all the rest of us. But there's some as don't. And strange to say, it's always them as does the bossing. Eh?'

But even stranger to say, Mr Boddington did not seem to have heard. He was staring at the parlour door with a peculiar expression on his face.

Chapter Five
MAKING THE WELKIN RING

Before anyone had time to comment, or perhaps even notice, the parlour door flew open again with a bang. My mother, her hair awry, her face flushed, appeared like a fury, wringing her hands in her apron.

'Oh Baxter, you *bad* ferret,' she screeched. 'You *silly* ferret! You bone-idle, halfwitted, worthless *apology* for a ferret! Now look what you've done!'

The embarrassed animals had no idea what to make of this outburst at all. I must admit that I was completely in the dark myself. Some of the younger ones tittered nervously, and there was a positive epidemic of coughing from the more tactful older ones. Mother didn't keep the mystery to herself for long.

'Look at the time, you bad lad! Look at the time,' she wailed.

I looked at the big round railway clock (rescued by my father from the LNWR dustbin at Willesden Junction on one of his trots around the country), and noted the position of the hands.

'Yes Ma,' I said, still baffled. 'It's—'

'It's twenty five minutes since that brew should have come off the fire, you daft haporth!' Mother bellowed. 'Call yourself a brewer? You're worse than our Dolly, and that's a fact.' No sense of justice at all, hadn't my old lady. She hadn't even *asked* me to time the boiling!

It was O.B. who saved the situation. He went boldly up to Mother and put his arm round her shoulders.

'Come on now, Daisy, don't fret. We've plenty of strong lads here. Have it off the fire and into the vat in half a jiff, you see if we don't. Then you and your silly Baxter can get the next lot on. No harm done.'

Mother sniffed forlornly, but she was extremely mollified. 'Well, if you think so... If you could really help...'

'Of course we can,' cried O.B. 'Nothing simpler. I tell you what – an even better idea. Four or five of the stronger ones can help you and Baxter, and me and Harrison, plus old Sherwood and Wilson there, we'll get the music going in the parlour.' He paused. 'If we have your permission, ma'am, that is? To raise the welkin a little in your delightful best room?'

'Oh dearie me!' said Mother, overwhelmed by such a polite attention. 'Well, I... If you...'

O.B. struck while the iron was hot. He bowed deeply, lifted up one of her paws, and pressed his lips to it. Then he picked up his canvas bag, signalled the musicians to follow, and marched into the parlour. As the door swung to we heard him still the hubbub with a shout.

'Now ladies, clear a space. The dancing is about to commence!'

Even before I'd formed three or four of the lads into a lifting team, Daisy was back in the land of the living. She pushed me to one side, all bustle and go to hide her blushes, and reorganized the whole shooting match. Within minutes she and her band of sweating conscripts were too absorbed to notice me. I slunk into the parlour, waiting for a lull in the music so that the opening of the door would not be so obvious, and joined the party.

In those days, home-made music was the rule, not the exception. And fortunately, us Wild Wooders was blessed with a natural talent that made us the envy of other animals. O.B., I can tell you, would certainly never have starved all the time his fingers was as nimble as they were that night. He had two or three concertinas, all London-made, one of them with hand-cut silver end-plates engraved with a scene of angels and devils chasing each other among the rows of buttons. Tonight he was playing his baritone Wheatstone, a very rare and beautiful instrument that he had off a Gypsy, fifteen bob down and no questions asked. This was deeper than the usual run of concertinas, but it blended in beautiful with Harrison's penny whistle.

That dour animal played like a ferret possessed. It completely changed his nature, putting a whistle between his lips. His scowly face cleared like a summer sky after a shower, his shoulders swayed from side to side, and his tail swished like a metronome. He'd picked it up off an Irish cousin, and had all the runs and trills and slurs off perfect.

The bass element was provided by Wilson, who played on that traditional seafarers' instrument the melodeon, or button accordion. The Lord knows how many thousands of miles of bucketing ocean voyages had given it its shape and condition, but the buttons, worn loose with fingering, clicked rhythmically as he played, rather like an old set of false teeth, while the upper registers were practically unusable. Which was ideal, as the booming deep notes set off the shrillness of the other players to perfection.

No country band would be complete without a violin, and that noble instrument was handled by the old stoat called Sherwood. The peculiar stance adopted by a fiddler, head down, chin tucked well in, was accentuated by his habit of staring at his flying fingers to get the positioning right, coupled with his funny eye. Sherwood, thus bent almost double, alongside the equally ancient and grey-furred Wilson pulling and pushing at the wheezing and whistling collection of holes and patches he called his bellows, was a sight for sore eyes.

It was in full swing when I slipped through the door, which was a pity from my point of view, because all the girls was already partnered. Still, it was nice to watch them at it, whirling and stamping, with their skirts swaying out and giving an odd glimpse of scarlet petticoat and trim ankle.

The first tune was fast and noisy, to set the tone for the evening, so a lot of the older dames were sitting it out looking with some disapproval, it must be said, at their husbands (greybeards, many of them) who were footing it among the younger spirits as though they'd never heard of age. I couldn't hear what was being said on account of the music, but from the pursed lips and shaken heads it couldn't have been far off 'Look at that silly old ferret; making a fool of himself as usual.' But then, most of the ladies had been sipping nothing but cordial all evening if you recall; and so must be forgiven, I suppose.

After the first dance there was a hubbub of clapping and cheering, and a general shout for something 'lively.' O.B., cheerful as ever despite the buckets of sweat pouring down his forehead and dripping off his long nose, shouted back at them: 'Lively! Lively! Why you impudent animals, that was the liveliest tune in the world!'

Ever ready to rise to a challenge, though, he went into a huddle with his fellow players. I saw old Wilson shake his head a bit dubious-like, but there was no stopping O.B. He pulled off his bright cravat and his plum-coloured waistcoat, loosened the top buttons of his shirt, and wiped his hand on his breeches.

'Take your partners then, my friends,' he announced. 'For something extra special. It'll make that last jig seem like a funeral march!'

Some of the respectable wives made frantic signals to their old fellows to duck out at this, and one or two even went over the floor and tugged at their sleeves. Quite the wrong thing to do, as nothing could be better calculated to make a stubborn animal stubborner. When the first chord was struck, the wives had to scuttle pretty sharpish to avoid being run down by the melee of dancing and swinging legs and arms. Naturally, none of the partnerships broke up, so I was left out in the cold.

Well, O.B. certainly kept his promise. He chose an old reel called The Gaping Goose, and after a few bars you could see why. Sherwood nearly turned himself upside down trying to follow his flying fingers with his funny eye, while Harrison Ferret became positively jovial, his tail a yellowish blur. O.B. himself went into a sort of trance of concentration. His racing fingers and swinging arms made a pattern in the hot air that matched the galloping music, and his heavy black boot crashed up and down tirelessly, driving the musicians and dancers mercilessly onwards. I could have kicked myself for missing it.

As two of the sets raced across the crowded parlour, they left a wide pathway between them. It was only open a second, but through it I saw another young fellow, another wallflower, on the other side of the room. It was Boddington Stoat, and looking very glum. Ah well, I thought, might as well play the good host. So I edged myself round the outside of the heaving throng, hopping in time to the music in spite of myself, and plonked my back against the wall alongside him.

'Hello, Boddington,' I shouted. 'You miss your chance too, did you? Old Daisy and her rotten brewing. They'll never play another like this, won't the boys, and there's nothing I likes better than a real fast number with a pretty girl.'

Boddington did not even answer. He just treated me to another dose of his cold and wintry smile – more a slight curling of the lips – and went back to gazing gloomily at the dancers. Well, I thought. That's not very chummy. So being in an expansive mood, and thinking happily of the sweating gaggle in the kitchen doing my hard work for me, I had another go.

'You're not looking too cheery, if I'm not being impolite to mention it. Is there anything the matter? You ought to have a Brewday, you know. Do you a power of good. What's up, old chap?'

This one really was a most peculiar animal, even for a stoat. They tend to be the most serious-minded of the three of us, and to be quite honest, somewhat short on humour and a sense of fun. Some say it's because they're smaller in general than us ferrets, and resent it, and envious of the weasels because *they're* smaller still, but always seem to come out on top. But for all their being a trifle hard to get on with, most of them are jolly fine blokes when you get into them, who certainly couldn't be called killjoys. Boddington however, seemed to be a different kettle of fish and no mistake. He appeared to look straight through me, frowning. Then he mouthed 'Nothing, nothing,' very irritably indeed. He turned his grey, scrunched up little face back to the swaying mass of bodies.

I must admit I allowed myself an oath – silent, I hasten to add – to the effect that he could go hang himself, and followed his gaze to the dancers. Strangely enough Dolly came whirling by at this exact instant, on the arm of a young ferret of considerable build. He was swinging her round vigorously, and both her feet were in fact off the ground, her gay petticoat swirling. As they shot past us, she darted a very saucy and challenging glance in our direction – which certainly wasn't meant for me! I sensed that Boddington had become very tense and nervous. I peeped sideways. Sure enough, he seemed transfixed, his front teeth sticking out slightly from his lips. As I peered, the tip of his tongue shot out and flicked over them. Well well well, I thought. That stuck-up stoat's took a shine to our Dolly!

Now, I was in a distinctly merry and thoughtless mood, what with the noise and the fun and the food and the barley wine, so I couldn't keep my silly thoughts to myself to save my life. I nudged the glowering, grey-suited animal coarsely in the ribs and yelled: 'Pretty, eh, our Dorothy? Broken many a young stoat's heart, has that little miss!'

He turned upon me instantly, and bellowed back (not in anger but because anything less was impossible in the throbbing parlour): 'What are you talking about, you idle ferret? What do you *imagine* you're talking about!'

So I thinks: 'Playing hard to get, eh, Mister Holier Than Thou Boddington Stoat?' And I blunders on.

'Well I wouldn't bother yourself if I was you, Mr B,' I roared. 'Our Dolly's quite tall for her age' – which was a totally unforgiveable and shameful reference to his shortness, even for a stoat – 'and anyway, she likes a bit of jollity about an animal!'

The little sharp-faced fellow was staring at me with bright red eyes. I felt my ears begin to burn and my heart begin to flutter with the terrible things I had said. Rudeness and lack of hospitality is an awesome sin among us animals, and I'd gone the whole hog. Being young, foolish and perhaps tipsy – although I don't offer that as an excuse – I was unable to do anything, think anything, or say anything that didn't make it worse. I giggled nervously, with a great hollow feeling inside me, and shrieked: 'Now if you was a richer animal. A gay dog like Mr Toad, for instance. Why, Dolly might enjoy a jaunt in your motor—'

I got no further. At that moment two things happened, that made my shame complete. Unnoticed by me in my flustered state, the band had been sawing and wheezing frantically to the end of The Gaping Goose. As the last chord crashed out, Boddington Stoat raised both his arms above his head in an absolute paroxysm of fury, and yelled, 'How *dare* you! Mr *Toad?* How *dare* you!' He pitched his shout to reach me through the music, but the music had stopped. His voice, strangled and shrill, echoed round the parlour. All the normal noise that one gets after a dance, the gruntings, the pantings, the laughter, the applause – all were absent. His voice rang round the room, and shook the Crown Derby china on the sideboard.

Both of us realised at once what had happened. We stood staring at each other, our faces crimson. The silence was electric.

You could have cut it into chunks and put it in your pocket. After a short pause the older animals again tried a rescue; a burst of chatter and coughing rose suddenly, filled the room, then died. One of the young ladies – a weasel I think, from her pitch – tittered and was shushed down. I swallowed hard, and tried to save the situation. I stammered:

'Mr Boddington. I... I...'

But Boddington did not stay for more. He turned on his heel and stalked across the room. I noticed, for no reason at all, that his boots squeaked. The door opened and closed. Still there was an uncanny, excruciating silence. I still think to this day that it might have gone on forever, for there truly seemed no way on earth of ending it. I was saved, in fact, by pure luck. Sherwood, tinkering uneasily with his violin, twisted one of the pegs. The E string, the highest, already overstrained from age and the extreme heat, broke with a twanging 'plink'. Again the young weasel tittered, and this time O.B. joined in.

'Oh, now that's torn it, Sherwood,' he shouted. 'Time for a rest and a wet. I'm as dry as a doughnut, anyway. Let's take a spell.'

He put down the Wheatstone and strode towards me. All the other animals, rather self-consciously, banged him on the back and thanked him for the music. He laughed gaily, and tried to put everyone at ease. Slowly people gathered in knots and started talking in low tones. O.B. put his arm round me.

'What's up, Baxter you dope? You look all hot and bothered. Had a bit of a row?'

I shrugged helplessly.

'I don't know, O.B., honest I don't. I was just having a laugh, like, with that queer stoat, and... Well, I saw him looking at our Doff, like... ' (Doff was Dolly, of course; another family name. Dolly, Doffy, Doff or Daw we called her.) 'Well, you know, him being a stoat and her a ferret and that. Well, I said he'd have to be a bit jollier for my silly sister, you know, take her a car ride or something, like Mr Toad say...'

I broke off, incoherent and miserable. O.B. laughed grimly.

'Toad, eh? Now *that's* a name you shouldn't mention when Boddington's around. Doesn't like friend Toad one little bit, doesn't Boddington.'

'But why not?' I asked, interested in spite of myself. 'I mean, Toad's a menace, and he's got more money than sense, and so on, but after all's said and done...'

O.B. hugged me tighter.

'I wouldn't be so sure about that, Baxter my lad. I've been wanting to have a little chat. You see, Boddington's got this idea... And I think he's right. There's going to be trouble here soon. Big trouble. And Toad's—'

But here, O.B. was cut off. The door flew open, and in came my mother. She was hot, steamy, and bewildered; which wasn't helped when she saw the guests whispering in little uncomfortable groups. She hurried over to me and whispered, 'Baxter boy, what's up? That stoat? What's the matter? Where's the music, the dancing?'

I shrugged miserably. I hadn't even got it right about Boddington having a fancy for my sister. I'd made a complete, a total, fool of myself. And O.B. was on his side; thought something serious was happening. My ma took one look at my face and gave me up as a bad job. She turned to O.B.

'Oh, Mr Weasel,' she said. 'Can't you do something? What will the guests think? Couldn't you strike up another jig, please? I'm sure they'd all be so happy if you could.'

O.B. patted her on the shoulder.

'Well, Mrs Ferret,' he replied. 'I don't think that would be just the thing right at this moment. I think we've pretty well danced ourselves to a standstill. Perhaps if someone could sing a nice, quiet song?'

Mother smiled at him, imploringly.

'Oh Mr Weasel, it would be a great honour if *you* would perhaps... '

But O.B., although famed throughout the Wood as a singer and composer, was not to be drawn. It was a rest he needed, and he knew that anything jolly would only unsettle everyone more.

I had a sudden inspiration. Dolly was a very fine hand at our old upright piano, and had a sweet, sad voice. I had a rush of affection for her, too, after having cast her, in my own mind at least, as the leading lady in such a drama of passion, without so much as a shred of sense, justice or reason. I would make up for it by letting her restore the party to happiness and calm.

'It's all right, Mother,' I said loudly. 'I've just had an idea, don't fret. Dolly must sing to us and play the piano. I'm sure everyone would like that.'

There was a general chorus of pleasure, cut off abruptly and painfully by the ringing, singing sound of my mother's hard old palm catching me a hearty crack around the head.

I squawked loudly, but Mother was much louder.

'You daft young bumpkin,' she roared. 'Why do you think I came barging in like that? Your sister's howling her heart out in the kitchen. And I want to know the reason why!'

After that the gathering broke up very rapid. And for all her promises that I wasn't too big to get a good larruping despite my age, my mother was much too depressed about the ruined evening to be bothered giving me one.

Chapter Six
BAXTER MEETS HIS MADMAN

The next time I saw O.B. and pals again it was several weeks later, and winter had settled in with a vengeance. Work on the farm had turned into a bitter pattern of listening to the complaints of the beasts – mainly about the cracks, leaks and draughts in their byres, sties and stables – and doing something about them. It was outdoor work, often, and I was always miserable cold. For although the farmer was a kind-hearted enough fellow, for them days, that didn't add up to much. Even when I could work from my little shed over in one corner of the yard, there was never any suggestion of heating in it – come rain or sleet, hail or freezing wind.

My main complaint about the bad weather, though, was to do with the Squeezer. As I've already said, the farmer was certain sure that I had to become an expert in every detail of that waggon; driving, maintenance and engineering. But he also had this strange idea that such an expensive item of machinery ought to be looked after like the best tea-set. That included not getting it wet if at all possible, rubbing it down like a prize horse if its paintwork *did* just happen to get splashed, and not driving it about in the cold, especially if there might be snow in the air.

Up to now the snows hadn't started, fortunately, although it was bitter cold a lot of the time, but that didn't impress the gaffer at all. When I'd gone through my morning routine of checking, polishing, setting and frankly standing about mooning because I wanted to feel that dazzling great machine throbbing with life all around me, along he'd come, slapping his big red hands on his cord jodphurs and breathing steam like one of Tetley's traction engines. He'd look at the lorry, say 'Well done, Ferret. You've brought her up like new again. Well done,' and stare up into the sky as though trying to surprise the moon in her daytime lodgings.

I'd stop breathing, practically, and stand beside him, my hands behind my back so that he couldn't see me wringing them like some old grannie. And morning after morning, he'd shake his head, and hum and hah about such and such a cloud, and how his corns, or his rheumatics, or even his missus, was playing him up, which was a sure sign that snow was on its way. Sometimes I'd almost weep with frustration.

Looking back on it, I wonder how I ever got that lorry on the go enough times to learn to drive at all. But on those glorious, heady, happy occasions I *was* permitted to swing the great brass handle, I packed ages of experience into a few short hours. I concentrated so hard I used to end up dizzy, and when I'd put her away at last, and climbed down from the cab, I'd find that my knees were shaking and there were spots before my eyes.

Each trip was connected with a specific job, so in a short time I had to cope with a very wide range of situations and conditions. Driving on hard, well-made roads, for instance, then swinging off onto cart tracks, followed by rolling, bumping, roaring excursions over the fields themselves. I had to go up steep hills empty, bouncing and slipping, then come back down them full, fighting the bucking, jarring steering wheel and alternately stabbing at the brakes and the accelerator to try and keep control. It was hard work and frightening, because at first I was feeling my way, trying to get the hang of it, so to speak, and I knew pretty well that if I put one foot wrong, if I so much as scratched the paintwork, the glorious partnership, me and my Throgmorton Squeezer, would come to an abrupt end.

Like all the worst shocks, the moment when that partner ship actually *did* end came like a bolt from the blue. Saddest of all, it came at the time of my proudest achievement, the time of the gaffer's greatest trust in me, the time when the world seemed to be running smoothly along just to make me happy.

The day started famous, like. At first light, when I'd gone through my routine and just blown out my lantern, the master came puffing and blowing up to me. It was a bitter morning, with the wind shrieking in from the north east, and ominous banks of clouds nudging upwards from the northern horizon. I hardly even considered the possibility of starting her up or going anywhere, and I'd persuaded Mother to let me wear my next week's woolly vest as well as the current one, because I had a shrewd suspicion I'd be up on a roof somewhere, or mending the well, or some equally bone-chilling chore. Gaffer looked very cheery though, wrapped up in a vast coat, steaming and puffing like a well-stoked locomotive.

'Well, animal,' he said. 'Is she ready to go? You've a long trip ahead of you today.'

My heart jumped. A trip! It was unbelievable!

'Yes, Gaffer,' I stammered. 'She'm all polished and raring to start. But begging your pardon, though' – for I too had my lovely lorry's best interests at heart, despite my own desires – 'Begging your pardon, don't you think it might not look like snow?'

The unpredictable farmer snorted, contemptuous like, as though such a remark just showed how craven a ferret I was.

'Snow! Well, and what if it does? If you can't handle the vee-hickle in a little drop of thick weather, young feller-me-lad, you're not much use to me, now are you?'

I blushed, despite the unfairness of this remark.

'Just thought, like, master, that the Throgmorton might get a mite mucked up. If—'

'Rubbish, boy, get her started and away. If it snows and she do get mucky, can't you clean her? Ain't that what I pays you good wages for? And besides' – he looked at me very fierce, all red cheeks and bushy eyebrows – 'Besides, my lad, seems to me neither of you am doing enough to maybe earn that keep. I've still to pay you if you do nothing all day long, and this here machine cost me a pretty penny just to lie there in its shed like Queen of Sheba. By Jingo, it's a lorry, not a porcelain statuette! Get it started and no more words or I'll clout your cheeky head!'

He'd worked himself up into quite a lather, so I said not another word. Just touched my cap and leapt for the safety of the cab. I scampered up, choked her, set my advance, switched on the fuel tap, then jumped to the ground to start her up. Up with the bonnet, prime the carburetter, chuck the face beneath its chin all friendly and excited like, and grab that great brass handle. Bang! Away first time. I let go the handle (in them days it was fixed, and stuck proudly out from the bottom of the radiator grill for all to see), scuttled back into the cab, reset my spark for tickover on the advance-retard lever, adjusted the choke, and listened happily as the Squeezer warmed herself up. The gaffer thrust his face into the cab, impressed in spite of himself.

'Well well, you've certainly got a way with her, boy,' he said. 'Started like an angel, even though it's cold enough to freeze brandy.' He pulled a piece of paper from his coat pocket, and handed it to me. 'You're to go to the town and fetch this. Hopkinson's woodyard. Ton and a half of cut timber. He'll be expecting you and it should be ready. Now, you drive careful, and you drive slow. It's a long way, and I want my truck and my timber back in one piece.'

The town! What a job! It was a good ten mile away, over real public roads. I positively glowed with pride.

The drive was like a beautiful dream. Although it was crisp and the Squeezer was pretty chilly, having no side glass nor heater, I was well wrapped up, extra vest and all. The sky was grey and metallic, and the early wind was dying down somewhat, although it still gusted. The roads were deserted, apart from the odd cart and Gypsy van. I truly revelled in it.

In the town, of course, things were different. Crowds all over the place, pony carts darting here and there, little kids running out in front of you without a thought in the world. I must allow I was a shade terrified at first! But although I felt I had to be all eyes and ears to avoid a collision, the mighty Squeezer commanded a great deal of respect because of its size, weight and hoarse klaxon. And the skill I'd collected on and around the farm was no flash in the pan. After a short time I knew I was in complete control. The lorry and the driver were like one. We moved together, stopped together, seemed to think together. Almost before I realised it, I'd found Hopkinson's, helped load the planks, made my mark on the docket of receipt, and was out on the open road again, heading for the low smudge on the rapidly darkening horizon that showed where the Wild Wood began.

To get to the farm by the main road meant skirting a large sticking-out lump of the Wood, and it occurred to me as I ground slowly along by it that if I made a small detour I could stop at Wilson's store and pick up some flour and stuff which I knew my mother had ordered. If I collected it in the Squeezer I could use one of Gaffer's barrows to push it home, and return the barrow tomorrow morning. It would save a three mile walk on Sunday, but truth to tell, I also rather fancied the idea of arriving at the old rat's shop in the waggon. There was usually one or two of the locals having a yarn and a game of dominoes round his pot-bellied coke stove, and sometimes even some of the younger Wild Wooders who happened not to be busy. I reckoned it would create quite a stir to pull up there and show off.

Accordingly, I kept my eye open until I saw the track – it was very secret and only one of us would have known it – and swung the Squeezer off the metalled road into the dim,

lofty avenue of cold bare trees. In no time at all I pulled to
a halt outside the great hollow oak stump that Wilson called
home (and work, for that matter!), hauled on the handbrake,
switched off the engine, and entered.

As the bell jangled, I was greeted by a chorus of shouts. 'It's
Baxter!' 'Why, you daft ferret, you had us all in a sweat!' 'We
thought there was something up!' 'Are you in a truck or is that
thunder?' For the animals had heard the sound of the engine, a
rarity indeed in them parts, and been half excited, half terrified
as to what it might mean. If O.B. had not been there, I expect
they would have all run into the back room and hid. But that
stout and intelligent animal had half guessed at once. Soon
they'd all crowded outside and admired the big and shining
waggon, prodded its solid tyres, patted the gleaming bonnet,
wondered aloud at its enormous load.

As we trooped back in again, O.B. detailed several of the
younger ones to go off. I heard something that sounded like
'See if Mr Boddington needs you,' then they were gone into
the gathering gloom. O.B. took me by the arm and guided me
to the place of honour by the stove, calling for a fresh cup of
tea from the sea rat. Two minutes later we all three sat down to
a huge earthenware pot of the steaming liquid, and a plate of
hot buttered scones straight from the oven. We munched and
sipped in silence for a short while, while I enjoyed the feeling
of life coming back to my chilled extremities. It was old Wilson
who spoke at last.

'Anyway,' he said to O.B., as though continuing a discussion from the point where my arrival had broke it off, 'I
think young Boddington's right. It's gone on long enough, and
it's gone on far enough.'

He took a last swig of tea from his thick china mug, and wiped his whiskers with the back of his horny old paw. O.B. chewed thoughtfully at a scone.

'Maybe,' he said, at last. 'But I can't help but think he's taking it all too serious, though. I mean, after all, they haven't done us any harm. I mean, all right, they're a bit above themselves, they cause a bit of a nuisance thinking they're the very thing, but they've not actually done us no *harm*.'

'You're wrong, you're wrong,' snapped the grey old sea rat, rather bad-tempered like. 'The way they carry on's enough. It just makes life harder for us. I say this: What do people say when they see lazy, idle fellows with more money than sense making exhibitions of themselves? Eh? That Rat bloke, for instance. Never done a hand's turn, always out and about in a blazer and a fancy cap, expensive little lightweight rowing boat – well how do you think that reflects on the rest of us rats? I was a seafarer for more years than—'

O.B. wagged his finger cheerily.

'Oh come on now, Wilson! You're just jealous, that's all. Granted you had to work for your living when you were at sea, but surely you wouldn't turn down the chance of a boat of your own to dabble about in? I think—' But the door bell jangled then, and an old bent squirrel came in for her weekly order. Wilson went behind the counter. I smiled at my friend.

'What was that all about?' I asked. 'Not like Wilson to get so het up. Sounded like politics rearing its ugly head!'

O.B. laughed, and poured me another cup of tea.

'Something like that. Ever since Boddington came to live in the Wild Wood it's been in the air. Now everyone seems to be having a go. They're right really, I suppose, but well, you know me. I like to get along with people if I can. Be friendly, have a chuckle. Everyone's got their little ways, but if they don't bother you…'

He sank his teeth into a fresh scone. I weighed up whether I should say what I was thinking or keep my mouth shut, but I was never one to consider anything that careful, so I went ahead.

'Where *is* your friend Boddington?' I asked (and I felt myself going red as I spoke). 'I haven't seen him since…well, since that night.'

'*My* friend,' laughed O.B. 'Well he certainly isn't yours, and that's a fact! He was all for punching you on the nose after that, but I told him not to be such an idiot. But my my, Baxter, you managed to rub him up the wrong way, and no mistake.'

I smiled ruefully.

'All by mentioning Mr Toad, you said at the time. Is that really so? Surely it can't be?'

'There you are, you see,' said O.B. 'That's the whole thing. It's the old, old friction between the River Bankers and us lot. But now Boddington's arrived, along with what looks like being another pretty hard and hungry winter, things seem to be coming to a head.'

I took another scone (O.B. was paying, after all), and sat back to listen. O.B. had no need to go over the old details, which we all knew only too well. The River Bank was where the smart set lived. Not all of them were exactly rich, but it was hard for us not to notice that while we all worked our fingers to the bone to keep a roof over our heads and a bite of food in the larder, they did very little that wasn't directly connected with pleasure and leisure. The group centred around a rich and indolent gentleman by the name of Toad, who lived in a vast, elegant and ancient house on the very edge of the river. He had everything that money could buy, and indulged his whims and fancies in a way that sometimes made a hard-working animal feel more than a little bitter. Even his especial friend, a dreamy, poetical sort of water rat, got a little embarrassed by Toad's excesses from time to time, although his own style of living was hardly what could be classed as austere. He had a very well-appointed and comfortable riverside hole, kept a couple of servants, ate and drank plainly but without stint, and did nothing from one day to the next but swim, boat, fish, go on picnics, or ramble over the surrounding countryside with his chums.

'What Boddington's saying,' O.B. told me earnestly, 'is that they're getting worse. There's this chap Mole, now. He's gone to live with Rat, and he's becoming part of the whole idle set-up. Why, last year he was just an ordinary sort of bloke with a little house and a cheery word for anyone. Now he's one of Toad's greatest pals, goes on caravan trips with him, dines at Toad Hall, and's full of airs and graces. Never had a servant in his life, nor dreamed of it neither, and now he's a River Banker through and through.'

There was a lot more in this vein, and I was quite interested, I must admit. Boddington thought Badger, a dour, grizzled old chap who actually lived in the Wild Wood, although he kept himself very much to himself, was letting us down by siding with Toad and his well-to-do cronies, and that it was time we showed them all that we was animals, too, as good as they were, and not to be walked all over.

'But O.B.,' I said. 'That's the part I don't get. I mean *are* we being walked all over? Seems to me nothing's changed at all. They've always been rich, we've always been poor. I suppose if any of us ever found the crock of gold at the end of the rainbow we'd go and buy a place like Toad's and join the River Bankers, too. You must admit, it's a fine house. And a diet of champagne and caviare wouldn't take much getting used to, even for a ferret like me, raised on bread and dripping.'

This argument got home to O.B., I could tell. He went dreamy for a while, and I think he was having a vision of himself being served vintage port out of a cut-glass decanter by a butler in livery. But he soon shook it off.

'It's the latest thing that's worst,' he said seriously. 'What upsets Boddington – who comes from a very poor family, bear in mind – is the way Toad's throwing away his money now. It's the motor car craze. Do you know how many machines that reckless animal has destroyed in the last few months? Well, do you?'

I didn't, neither did I speak. For try as I might, Toad's latest fad – which others found so terrible, apparently – I could only think of in terms of sheer envy.

It had started, so the story went, while Toad and a couple of his leisured friends were making a trip in a horse-drawn caravan of the Gypsy type (although no Gypsy would have recognised it, so chintzy, spotless and respectable had it been made to suit River Bank tastes). One afternoon, ran the legend, a motor car had appeared over the horizon at speed, rushed past the van in a cloud of dust and exhaust fumes, and frightened the horse so much that he'd backed the van into a ditch. Instead of attempting to prosecute, Toad had decided that the thing for him was to buy a motor car himself! If I was to be honest, I suspected I would have done exactly the same, given half a chance.

O.B. was talking. I don't know how much I'd missed, but it was something to the effect that it was a terrible sin for all that good money to be hurled away when so many animals could put it to such good use. And it was dangerous to boot.

Sometime soon, Toad was going to do someone a serious hurt. Why, said O.B., he'd already been in hospital three times himself. Drivers were a menace, he said, an absolute menace. And Boddington said something should be done about it.

Frankly, I was getting a little tired of the grey and bilious Boddington. Especially now he seemed to be starting a one-man crusade aimed at us motorists. I took a deep breath.

'Well I must say, O.B., that I think it all sounds silly. We've always had our differences with that lot, true enough. But Toad's a jolly enough old fellow and a sight more pleasanter than *some* folks with money. Live and let live is my motto, and I've always thought it was yours as well, like.'

And I stood up deliberate, and reached for my coat and muffler.

O.B. sucked at his teeth thoughtfully.

'You might be right, Baxter, you might be right. I've always got on with 'em, true. But Boddington's got a point, you know. He's having a meeting with some of the others this afternoon, that's where those youngsters went when you came in. He's examining ways and means. Ways and means of doing something about it.'

I tucked in my muffler ends, and buckled my belt.

'Live and let live, I say. He's done us no harm that I know of, nor his friends neither.'

O.B. shook his head.

'As Boddington says – mind, he's agin you anyway – but as he says, you're in work and you've not got much to worry about. You might be a little more aware – that's his word for it – if you had something to fear from the winter. If you got the sack you'd change your tune.'

He grinned broadly at me.

'That's what he says, my boy, the miserable old stoat. Young Baxter needs a spot of hardship to make him realise whose side he's on!'

I just snorted. The cheek of it! That insolent and mean-minded animal, dipping his great long whingey nose into my affairs. My eye caught Wilson's American wall clock, and it brought me up short.

'Blimey, O.B.! Look at the time. That dippy Boddington'll see his dream come true if I'm not careful. I'm meant to be doing a job, not talking nonsense over a tea-kettle. I'd better shift before the gaffer gives me the boot.'

I shouted to the sea rat, who was still wandering about the great open bins and sacks of produce in the cluttered shop getting the old lady's order ready. 'I'm off then, Wilson. I dropped in for that couple of hundredweight of stuff for my ma, but I'll have to come back some other time. All right? Cheerio.'

'You young chatterbox,' he called back. 'It's a wonder you ever get anything done.'

'Hark who's talking then,' I laughed. 'Cheerio all.' And I walked over to the stout door and hauled it open.

'Cripes! It's snowing!'

The other animals crowded over and we silently watched the big flakes falling heavily to the already whitened ground. It gave us pause for thought. Snow was never welcome, except to children and the odd daftie like my old father had been. With the truck to worry about I relished it even less.

I said goodbye again more cheerily than I felt, and climbed into the cab to set my controls. The door handle was icy and the starting handle was even worse. But I chucked the little chin and she roared into life first swing. It had gone from daylight, through dusk to pitchy night while we'd been guzzling tea and scones, so I had to light the big lamps. With my finger ends only half burnt to cinders, I popped back into the cab, wiped the plate-glass screen, and set off.

The drive along the woodland track was pretty hair-raising. The dim lights were made dimmer all the time by snow settling on the thick curved lenses. Huge shadowy tree trunks seemed to step out of the moving curtain of snow that trembled and shook in the yellow glare. I'd think I was dead centre and safe, when I'd suddenly be aiming slap bang into a cold wet trunk. Every time I braked, the wheels would lock in the watery, muddy layer of ice under the smooth, solid rubber tyres. Then I'd have to back cautiously – and blindly – into what I thought was the main track once more, and grind slowly off in bottom gear. I had, as well, to keep my head out of the side window for the improvement in vision it gave me, so very soon my whole face was frozen; cheeks, nose and chin.

After what felt like an age I reached the edge of the Wood. As the trees ended the sky became a little brighter, the snow swirled less wild, life rapidly got more worth living. I looked carefully both ways, although in those days, in those parts, traffic was almost non-existent. Only a madman, in any case, would be out and about on a night like this. All clear. I eased out the clutch and drove slowly off the narrow track onto the safety and comfort of the hard, metalled road.

I didn't hear a thing at first. There was a sudden, heart-wrenching glare of lights around the bend, a wild impression of something tearing towards me through the snow, then finally – noise. A screaming engine, squealing brakes, a raucous, lunatic poop-pooping of a horn. The car hit the lorry at the front, tore off the starting-handle, the radiator and one mudguard, bounced across the road like a rubber ball, glanced off a tree, skeetered back to the centre again and disappeared into the night.

I had met my madman.

As the noise of the Armstrong Hardcastle Mouton Special faded away I sat in the cab of the assassinated Squeezer and cried. The noise of my sobs, the steam escaping from the shattered radiator, the hot engine cooling down: these sounds were swallowed up in the pale, muffling blanket of the snow.

Chapter Seven
A CHIVVYING UP

My last job for the gaffer before I took my much reviled and berated body out of his sight forever, was to go with Tetley the next day and haul the sad wreck of my pride and joy back to the farmyard.

The morning was clear, crisp and cold, with a thick carpet of sparkling, pristine snow. Old Betsy was on top of her form, hissing and clanking hotly as we trundled along the otherwise silent and deserted road. She obviously had some mechanical soul lurking in all those tons of black old metal, and her triumphant hour had come. She was to preside over the burial of her hated rival; drag the corpse of the twentieth century unprotesting back into the nineteenth. Tetley, though, a taciturn animal at the best of times, looked even more forlorn than usual, as though he deeply sympathised with me, the chief mourner, in my hour of loss.

Needless to say, it was all a matter of complete indifference to me, anyway. Nothing anyone could have done or said would have altered my state of mind on that beautiful, unnoticed daybreak. In one fell swoop my whole life was changed. Last evening I had been a happy, reasonably well off, contented family ferret, responsible and respected. Now I was a destitute, out-of-work, miserable and totally disgraced animal who could hardly hold up his head in decent company. The hard things the gaffer had said to me when I'd trudged into the farmyard in the black night were bad enough. But my mother's words when I'd got home had been worse. They'd burnt into my very soul.

She'd known at once, of course, that something dreadful had happened. In fact she appeared to know exactly what it was, which confused matters more than somewhat, as it left us talking at cross-purposes for a while. I'd hardly had time to get my hand on the knob before the front door was jerked open by a bright-eyed Saunders. He was beside himself with excitement and jumped up and down squeaking.

'Is there going to be a war?' he twittered, tugging at my scarf, and I was so tired and miserable that I'd have clouted his silly head myself, only Mother, as usual, got there first and sent him squalling into the kitchen. Then it was my turn, without warning or any justification that I could imagine. It started me off bawling again, old as I was, and I stood like a clump, tears dripping off my frozen snout, saying pathetically 'what was that for, Ma?' over and over again.

Daisy's answer, characteristically, was another clout, followed by some tirade to the effect that I shouldn't have got mixed up in such a thing, and it was a disgrace to self respecting animals, and if that O.B. Weasel so much as showed his face at our hole again it'd be the worse for him, important as his family was.

I struggled out of my outdoor clothes and let it wash over me, hardly bothering to wonder what she was burbling about. She went on wittering and wringing her hands all the way into the kitchen, and I went on bawling, and I could hear Saunders screaming somewhere in a corner, and one of the other kids was at it as well. Just to complete the picture of the happy family at rest and play, the first thing I saw when I opened the door is our Dolly sitting at the kitchen table all tragic-like, and *she's* wiping her eyes too, *and* sniffing, *and* shaking.

By this time Mother was running out of steam, and her lower lip was also looking trembly and uncertain-like, as though she was going to join the waterworks at any moment.

'Oh Baxter,' she wavered. 'You shouldn't't've been a part of it. It'll only cause trouble, you see if it don't. They've got influence, them folks, and what if you was to lose your job through it?'

'Mother,' I said, making a huge effort to control my heaving lungs for a minute, 'I don't know what you're talking about, I'm blowed if I do. But I've already... I've already... I've GOT the sack!' Then I just let out a huge howl and rushed into her arms and bawled like a baby.

Of course, Daisy came all over maternal then, and hugged me, and kissed me, and the little ones came out of their corners and stopped crying and looked on, round-eyed and silent.

Dolly, who seemed to dither less, and do more, almost by the hour these days, dried her eyes and set about making me a cup of tea. When the tempest died down a little she shooed the littluns off to bed, while Ma and me talked it out.

When something completely terrible had happened, my mother could always be relied on to become grave, and sensible, and intelligent. As she listened to my tale she didn't rant or rave, she didn't clout me, she didn't even tut tut. Just sat opposite me at the table, her tired old face drawn, sipping her tea. Dolly came back halfway through, and Ma mechanically pulled down another mug from the dresser and filled it from the big earthenware teapot in one silent movement. My sister, unexpectedly quiet and serious, parked herself in a cane-backed chair and watched my face as I spoke.

I told the story unvarnished, not going into detail, and not telling no lies. I knew I shouldn't have been in Wilson's and so did everyone else. I didn't try to make an excuse of the fact that I went for Ma's stores. When I'd more or less reached the end, it was Dolly who spoke first. She stared hard at me and two big tears squeezed themselves out of her eyes, one on each side of her sleek and pretty nose.

'Oh Bax,' she muttered. 'You haven't half gone and made a mess of things—'

My mother cut her off, not unkindly, with a sharp tap on the knee. She said the words that hurt so much more than Gaffer's, because they were so kind, and brave.

'You leave your brother alone, miss,' she told our Doff. 'He's had a bad day, and he don't need you to tell him about it.'

She picked up the teapot, weighed it, banged it down.

'Time for bed I reckon, my loves,' she said. 'Baxter's got to be up in the morning. No doubt but his master'll want to have a word or two before he's discharged, then he must try for another position.'

She smiled at me and moved her paw from Dolly's knee to my own.

'Get some sleep, son, you'll be needing it. Tomorrow's a new day, and things'll look better. You'll get another job perhaps, or perhaps you will not. But remember, Baxter. We'll be all right whatever happens.'

We'd all went to our beds then, and I'd slept deep and dreamless, for all I thought I wouldn't. But Ma was wrong on one score and that's a fact. When I'd woke up in the grey, chilling dawn, things hadn't felt no better at all. And when I'd looked at all them hungry mouths around the breakfast table, clamouring for their porridge, I'd felt my blood run cold.

But now Tetley was shouting at me above the noise of hissing steam, and I wrenched myself back to the present and looked around the still, white countryside. We weren't far off. With an effort I tuned in my earholes to the words that fought the clanking, battering noise of the traction engine, but I didn't quite understand them.

'Sorry, old friend,' I said. 'Didn't really catch all that; miles away I was. You know, one thing and another.'

His wisened old face grew serious.

'Never you mind, Baxter,' he said. 'You'll find something. Good worker you are, everyone knows it. Won't be long before you'm snapped up.'

I ventured a smile, although his words were hollow, I knew. 'Hope so,' I replied. 'But what was you saying, just now? I am interested, honest.'

'Oh, just about last night. Funny do, that. Start a muck of trouble my missus do reckon, but I ain't so sure.'

I must have looked puzzled, for Tetley then asked me if I knew about it, or if perhaps I'd been on the road and missed the whole thing. I remembered that my silly brother Saunders had said something about a war, then of course that Daisy had laid into me as soon as I'd got home for something I knew nowt about.

'Funny you should mention it, Tetley,' I told him. 'I thought something was up, but I never found out what. I must have been...' I tailed off. The old fellow was wound up with his story, however, and given the opportunity, went off like clockwork.

'Well, no one do know how it all started, like,' he said, 'but it seems like it was summat to do with one of them River Bankers. Then there was the meeting, too. I mean I didn't *go*, I couldn't could I, what with me working on the farm for Gaffer and all, but my lad Webster, he went along, although my missus do say as how his missus, a right sharp one she is that Sally, well she did try to stop him, says the whole thing would end in trouble, follow?'

He broke off on this question – for to give Tetley his due, he was aware that his method of telling a story often left his listeners deep in the wood of confusion – and I thought rapidly, with an added bit of guesswork.

'There was a meeting in the Wild Wood?' I said. 'Organised by that stoat Boddington? And your son Webster went to it but you didn't?'

Tetley gave me an admiring glance.

'You'm a sharp one and no mistake,' he replied. 'I couldn't've put it clearer meself!'

Then he went on: 'Anyway, my lad Webster, he told me all about it, see? Seems that while they're having this meeting – stoats, ferrets and weasels together, led by this lad Boddington – well, and he's a queer one says my boy, all angry and bitter, and on about the rich and the poor, and the cans and can'ts and the does and the don'ts or somesuch. Anyroad, he's all for us Wild Wooders doing something about it, like. My missus and Sally, you should have heard them! "Trouble trouble trouble," they bleated, like a pair of sheep, Webster got quite heated he did, follow?'

This was harder, but I sorted it out in the end.

'What happened in the meeting, then?' I said. 'You mentioned a River Banker. Surely one of them weren't there? At the meeting?'

'No no no no no, not a bit of it,' says Tetley, jumping up and down on the footplate. 'No, see, *during* the meeting, while the meeting's *on* like, in comes this young weasel, do you know him, young chap called JWL from over Greengate way, in he comes and says as how this River Banker, perhaps you know *him?* Feller called Mole, they do say as how he'm new there, used to live in the flats, the fields you understand, now lodges with Rat, you must know Rat, jolly fellow with the boat, see him in the Wood sometimes, nice feller?'

Yes I did know Rat, at least by repute, and I had heard of his friend Mole. How could I not have done, now this vexatious Boddington had come to live among us? But what had they *done?*

'Well,' I said, impatient-like. 'So young JWL busts in. Then what happens?'

Tetley smiled.

'Busts in. That's just exactly it, if Web's to be believed. There they all are, gassing away, and in "busts" JWL. You've a way with words, young Baxter. You'll be all right, a bright young feller like you. Don't you worry about this trouble, you'll soon be snapped up, don't you fret.'

He broke off and spun the wheel with practised hand, and Old Betsy wheezed and clanked as she lumbered heavily round a bend. I was bursting with impatience, but Old Tetley was a steam man through and through, and over the years the habit of slowness, everything taking an age to happen, had soaked into his very being. I breathed deeply and tried to absorb some of his monumental patience to cope with his monumental lack of hurry.

'Burst in like a safety valve a-blowing at all accounts,' the old fellow finally continued. 'And he yells out: "That Mole feller. He's a-coming this way! He's a-coming to the Wild Wood!" And it was so. There, so Webster told me, just as if it might be you talking to me now, as large as life in rubber shoes and a cap with a peak upon it, is this silly feller venturing into our Wood. And on a day when not even a dog should be about, as you'll well remember.'

I did, with a shiver despite the pulsating heat of the footplate. Well, this was most unusual. The River Bankers might have been rich, but they weren't mad. And there were some things in them days that animals just did not do. Winter's a strange time, and hunger's a peculiar thing, if not a funny one. A wood is a big, dark, lonely, dangerous place and ours was more so than most, whence perhaps its name. The Wild Wood was all sorts of things to all sorts of animals. To the River Bankers it was a distant and menacing area not to be ventured into lightly or alone.

'Billy Bingo,' I said. 'What a strange thing for him to do. That's just asking for trouble I reckon. What happened?'

'Well you'm dead right, young'un,' replied Tetley. 'Specially on account of how that sharp young stoat's been beefing and bellyaching these last few whiles. Caused an uproar it did, and some of the younger ones, stoats especial, being as how they, you know, well...'

I knew exactly what he meant, but I didn't say anything. I waited till Tetley found his thread again.

'Well 'tween you'n me, Baxter, if it hadn't been for the ferrets and weasels, there'd've been a proper nasty do on last night. As it was, that Mole chap come unstuck in no uncertain terms. The stoats, and they was in the majority, there being more of them than anyone else, follow, well, they was all for going the whole hog. General jumping and leaping about for coats and scarves and sticks and stones. 'Twould have been a dangerous thing to let get under way. You know how it is, Baxter. These things can easy get out of hand, follow?'

I followed only too well, but Tetley's roundabout way of telling a tale was driving me potty. We were approaching the last bend before the Throgmorton, and when we arrived we'd be too busy and I'd be too miserable, I had no doubt, to carry on the conversation.

'What did they do?' I asked, as casual as I could muster up. 'Did they attack him or what? What stopped the stoats, then?'

'Ah,' beamed Tetley. 'Good question as usual, young Baxter, you're smart you are, smart as paint. Well, it was mainly luck like, follow, so my Webster said. Two youngsters in particular spoke up agin it, on account it weren't the time nor place, they said. Said it would bring down the law on us, they shouldn't wonder. Said the Chief Weasel would have a thing or two to say on any such a thing. Ah.'

'Who were they? Anyone I know? I bet O.B. was one—' Oh no, he'd been with me in Wilson's. How strange.

'That fat feller what dances. Weasel. Bit of a namby pamby I've always thought he looked, but my Web said he spoke up like a good'un. Radcliffe is his name would it be? Danged if I know for sure. T'other one, anyway, that's easy. That gloomy ferret Harrison as is always jawing your leg off about guns. Can't understand the half of it I can't, not how an animal can always talk about one thing. My old lady now, she goes on about baking in much the same fashion. But I always consoles myself with the thought that when she's finished the actual event, her mouth'll be full of pastry, so silence at last; and mine too, eh, which can't be such a miserable thing, follow?'

His crooked, powerful old paw spun the wheel then, and Old Betsy commenced slowly to follow the curve of the road.

'Tetley,' I said. 'Tell me quick-like. What did they do? Did they catch him? Did they harm him? Did he get away?'

'Well, there was chivvying. Ah, there was surely that. And he certainly disappeared, like, that's a fact. And he was certainly posted as missing back on River Bank, on account of how that Rat feller turned up later a-looking for him. Armed to the teeth, he was, not such a fool as his silly young friend, eh? But as my Webster said last night when Sally, that's his missus you understand, was saying they shouldn't agone and done it, he says to her— Hello! Helloelloello! What's that, then? Look Baxter, by your poor old lorry!'

We had rounded the bend. Determined to try and hear the end of the tale I'd clenched my fists and kept my eyes on Tetley's clattering dentures rather than look up. Now I did. Alongside the dismal wreck, peering into the cab, was a figure.

'Thieves!' shrieked old Tetley. 'Robbers! Villains come to lay hands upon Gaffer's lawful timber!'

He banged open Old Betsy's throttle another fraction with a handy wrench, although she was already giving her very best speed. His free hand waved above his head till it contacted the whistle wire, on which he dangled frantically, one booted foot hovering in the air. A hoarse blast of sound and steam rent the clear and frosty morning.

The figure looked up, apparently not in the least alarmed.

He moved to the front of the Squeezer in fact, and lounged on the sagging bonnet, about where the mudguard should have been. He was waiting for us.

As we lumbered forward, it appeared that there was another vehicle parked beside the lorry, which we had not been able to see at first. It slowly came into view, took shape and colour. I felt my stomach begin to flutter, my fingers to tremble. It was a motor car. A battered motor car. A very severely battered motor car.

Old Tetley drove the last few yards in the grim silence of concentration. He eased the steam back, judging his distance to a tee. The huge engine ground and grunted to a halt only inches from where the Throgmorton's radiator used to be. There was a moment of absolutely uncanny quiet after the din, until the engine settled down to a contented and familiar hissing as she built up pressure.

The black-coated figure pushed himself upright with a leather-gauntletted paw and walked towards us.

'Hello, you chaps,' he said at last. 'What a splendid day.'

It was Mr Toad.

Chapter Eight
INSULT TO INJURY

Well truth to tell, it would have been impossible to find two more deeply flummoxed animals than me and old Tetley at that precise moment, if you'd searched the four corners of the globe. We was flabbergasted, amazed, struck dumb. The story of Mole was forgot – I didn't hear the end of it until that long and weary day was nearly done, by which time the weight of intervening events made it seem a mere nothing, or bagatelle as we used to say. We just stood there, on the quietly steaming traction engine, staring at the bizarre figure that looked up at us from the frozen roadway. After a while Tetley let out a sneeze, and me a 'Bless you', mechanical as clockwork. Then we all commenced to look at each other like dummies again.

Finally Toad raised a paw and pushed his big glass goggles up from his eyes onto the back-to-front cap he had on. He give us a smile that can only be described as cheerful-like, and said: 'Just tootled over to see the damage. Rum go, eh?'

We were still tongue-tied. Although we knew most of the people from the River Bank by sight, and a couple of them to pass the time of day with, to actually be faced with the rich and powerful Mr Toad in the flesh as it were, to be addressed by him, to be looking into his smiling – if uncommonly ugly – mug like, was not to be handled no how. What were we to say? Tetley had been a working man all his life and never moved more than five miles from his dwelling, even on a traction engine. I was a mere nobody, and a disgraced ferret to boot. Tetley sneezed again, I said 'Bless you' again, we became dumb again. Old Betsy, relaxing after her long haul, clanked once. Then silence.

Mr Toad seemed puzzled. He danced a sort of jig in the snow, as if to warm up his toes. He clapped his short arms around his fat body, encased as it was in rich leather down to the top of his furry boots. He gave a sort of laugh, more like a giggle you'd call it.

'Made a jolly good mess out of that, didn't I just,' he said at last, very gay, indicating the poor Squeezer.

Tetley and me went red by degrees. He seemed to be proud of it! He seemed to think he'd done a good deed! Still we could find nowt to say at all. Toad giggled again.

'Look at that, eh, you fellows. Must be tons of truck there, tons of it. Throgmorton, I believe. Not a firm I'd deal with, if you get my meaning. I like something tough. Something substantial. Something built to last. Why, one good collision, and look at it! Tinny! No other word for it. Just look.'

My eyes wandered to my lorry. The front was like a battle ground after a major engagement. Lights gone, radiator in pieces, the remains of the mudguard like the tattered ear of an old fighting dog. The offside wheel had been wrenched off its stub-axle, and during the night the weight of timber had pressed the nose of the lorry to the ground, so that it appeared to be kneeling.

Toad continued, getting more and more excited. He was smiling, actually smiling. He was enjoying himself!

'Now *my* machine. That's what I *call* a machine. Only a motor car' – He checked himself and chuckled – '*Only* a motor car! A motor car of the noblest. A masterpiece of the engineer's art. The finest thing that ever roared along on four wheels. Look at her.' And he swept an arm vaguely in the direction of his vehicle. 'Bent but beautiful, battered but unbowed, bashed but... but... But beautiful,' he ended, rather lamely.

Tetley muttered something. Toad looked expectant, not having heard, so Tetley muttered it again.

'We've come for the waggon. 'Tis the gaffer's.'

Mr Toad slapped the side of Old Betsy heartily, and the smell of scorched hide rose from his hastily retracted gauntlet.

'Good men, good men. Tow the old warhorse back to rest, eh? Just the fellows I wanted to meet. Give me the... er … the gaffer's name if you'd be so kind, so that I can get in touch and settle the account with him.'

I saw a glimmer of hope through my misery. Took my courage in both hands. Spoke to the gentleman.

'Would you be saying... ? I mean, does that allow that you...? How can I put it, I mean...'

It was no use. I was in a new world, a different world. I didn't even know how to speak the same language.

Toad jigged about again.

'Spit it out, my boy,' he said jovially. 'No need to be shy. No need to fear old Toad. I won't bite you, you can count on it. Gospel truth!'

It all came pouring from me in a rush, like a gushing mountain torrent.

'It was your fault!' I babbled. 'All your fault! That's the truth of the matter, although it's me what's got the boot and am in a fair old way to starving! There I was coming out of the lane doing no one no harm, not a care in the world, and WHAM, round you comes like a lunatic, begging your pardon sir, and what chance did I have ever to avoid you I'd like to know!'

I stopped, panting. Me and Old Betsy steamed together for a few moments.

Then I sniffed.

'Begging your pardon, sir. I'm not meaning to be rude, like. But that's how it was.'

The fat and jolly animal pushed his cap further back on his head, and whistled between his teeth.

'You!' he said. 'You! A young fellow like you driving that monster. I say, well done, *well* done!

'But come now,' he went on, crafty all at once. 'It can hardly have been my fault, how can you say such a thing? Main road, right of way, bowling along at a gentle jog to get home to my supper. Why—'

I let out a screech of disbelief.

'A gentle jog! Why sir, however can that be? Why Tetley, as you see me standing on this footplate, he were doing a hundred mile an hour or I'm a rabbit! A gentle jog! It was like my last moment on earth had come!'

Tetley lowered his eyes to his ashy old boots and only muttered unintelligibly. But Toad seemed to swell up in the most peculiar way. He was smiling so broad his funny flat face was almost split from ear to ear.

'A hundred miles an hour indeed,' he said dreamily. 'You foolish animal, it was nowhere in the vicinity of such a figure. Only a fool would drive so recklessly. Not that my motor car would be incapable, let me hasten to add. No no, my young friend, that vehicle there, that poem of grace and power, could do... well... a hundred and *twenty* miles an hour.' He looked a little uncomfortable, and added defiantly: 'With ease!'

'Be that as it may, Mr Toad,' I replied, greatly emboldened. 'But you was going too fast. I come out and I had no choice but be hit, and it's a crying shame!'

'Ah, my boy. Think of the joy, the value of the event. To be struck down by an Armstrong! To be vanquished by a Hardcastle! Many animals would give their tails for such an honour. There I was, bowling along in top *vitesse* at some sixty miles an hour. Visibility zero, roadholding worse than useless, lights hardly denting the snow, brakes a joke, merely. I drop into third to negotiate the bend. Give her a bit of stick to correct the slide. Accelerate hard as we straighten. Higher and higher go the revs, in clutch and thrust the gear lever into top again, out clutch and foot down... And suddenly I see you, trying to crawl out like a great slug! Oh joy! I accelerate! Can you escape? Of course not! Toad is invincible! Toad cannot miss! Ah, my boy—'

At this point the traction engine, having done no work for some time, reached full pressure and blew the safety valve. The surplus steam exhausted itself with an ear-splitting roar for several seconds, while Tetley and me stared at each other open-mouthed. Had we gone barmy, or had that fat unwieldy toad at our feet? Had he really said it? That he'd *tried* to hit me last night? When the safety valve shut again there was a pause while our ears readjusted themselves to the silence. Then Tetley, red-faced, muttered: 'I heard that, Mr Toad, begging your honour's pardon. A full confession, signed, sealed and delivered, as it were. Follow?'

'Pooh,' said Toad. 'What of it? I've had hundreds of such incidents. And you must admit, I came off best. Throgmortons, pah! Someone ought to write to the papers about them!'

'But I lost my job,' I shouted, enraged. 'When I got back, Gaffer fired me on the spot! I've a ma and six brothers and sisters to keep, and you think it's the cause for boasting!' He went red himself then, quite unexpectedly, and coughed.

'Oh,' he said. 'Yes, well. Well, I have heard of this sort of thing, of course. Yes. Brothers and sisters, eh? Hm. Most awkward.'

Tetley said bravely: 'Signed, sealed and delivered, see. Witnessed. Follow?'

Toad stamped his expensive boot on the ground angrily.

'Hold your tongue, my good man. I'm talking to the boy.'

A pause. Then:

'Boy,' he said grandly, 'this is what I'll do. You're obviously wasting your time on such tinny items as that luckless truck. If you care to pop round to Toad Hall some time, I'll see if I can't set you to work on my motor cars. Several of them I've got, naturally, in extensive and well appointed garage space. You can work on 'em, and mechanic 'em, and generally muck about, all right? Keep you off the streets, what, and put a bit of bread back in the breadbin. Good.'

Can you imagine how I felt? I was speechless. To hear my beautiful motor lorry, so woefully and savagely attacked without warning or chance of escape, described as tinny.

To be offered a sometime maybe job 'mucking about' with motor cars to 'keep me off the streets' after I'd spent so many years working so hard and so proudly for a good master who appreciated me. To be told lightly I could get a 'bit of bread' to keep my family going. I could not speak. I merely stuttered.

He smiled broadly and pulled down his goggles once more.

'There there, my young friend, don't bother to thank me now. Later will do, there's a good chap.' He made to go, but turned back.

'By the way, old timer,' he said to Tetley. 'Tell your master to send the bill to Toad Hall, will you? I'll settle, of course. Money's no object to Toad, I can tell you.'

We watched him disappear into the battered Armstrong Mouton Special. It had a shattered windscreen, only one light, and an offside front wheel that wobbled horribly. He crashed the gears, raced the engine, and let out the clutch so jerkily that the machine took off like a kangaroo hopping out of sight. I turned to my old friend.

'He can't even drive, look,' I told him. 'He can't even drive.'

Tetley patted me on the back clumsily.

'Will you go, young feller? For that job like, follow? Said you'd be snapped up, didn't I?' But he couldn't even raise a smile.

'Go there?' I said. 'To Toad Hall? I'd rather starve first. And that's a fact.'

Those were practically the last words we spoke that morning, for as the memory of our odd meeting dwindled along with the sound of that fat animal's dreadful gear changes and pooping horn, the memory of our purpose eased itself back into our minds. It was hard, slow work getting the lorry ready for the long haul back to the farm, and by the time Old Betsy was set to go, we was both about jiggered. Anyway, there wasn't much left to talk about, was there?

Back at the farm we unhitched the wreck in silence, and let it take up its sad kneeling position in the barn that it had filled so proudly until the day before. Tetley climbed back onto his engine, shaking his head. He opened his mouth, shut it with a snap, and just touched his cap to me instead. I, too, was unable to speak.

The gaffer, not unexpectedly, was nowhere to be seen. I shrugged my shoulders, put my hands deep into my pockets, started on the long trudge home.

Chapter Nine
A STORMY MEETING

Before I got halfway there, I changed my mind. As I was now out of work, and as it was much too late in the day to start thinking about looking for alternative employment, I might as well make myself useful in some other respect.

Like, for instance, going to Wilson's shop to pick up at least some of Ma's stores – which fortunately was already settled for – or even try and borrow a sledge and haul the lot. Truth to tell, I wasn't at all sure that I could face Daisy just at the present time. I had to find something constructive to do.

The evenings were drawing in with a vengeance, and the Wild Wood, bare and dank, was not a particular nice place to be wandering in, even for one like me, born and raised here. My mind kept turning to all sorts of things as I walked through the secret, silent ways. Not least that poor bloke Mole. What he must have felt like I could scarce imagine, lost and alone; but what a thing to do, eh, come on his own? As I approached Wilson's door I pushed the subject to the back of my mind. Odder still to think on this warm and friendly general store. Only the very last afternoon I'd pulled my Squeezer to a halt here and taken tea and cake with great happiness. In the meantime I felt as if I'd aged twenty years. I found myself hoping against hope that there'd be none of the animals I knew best here, excepting for Wilson, that is.

Fat chance of that I must say! As I pushed open the door a wave of hot air and a babble of urgent conversation rushed out to meet me. I tried to close it again and slip away unseen, but I had been spotted. Roly Poly Radcliffe bounced over and seized me by the arm. His eyes were shining with excitement, and he had to shout over the hubbub of voices to make himself heard.

'Hello Baxter, old boy. You look frozen. Come in and warm up before the fun starts.'

I started to rip off my heavy coat, for the number of animals crammed into the dark, aromatic shop made it very hot indeed, and I'd started to sizzle and sweat the moment I was dragged over the threshold. As I got my outer clothes off I panted, 'What fun? What's going on, Radcliffe? Why is everyone here like this?'

It seemed, in fact, that everyone *was* at Wilson's this cold, bleak afternoon. Over by the stove I caught a flash of plum velvet – O.B.'s waistcoat, for a shilling – and I also spotted

Harrison in earnest conversation with a grey-suited figure that could only be the stoat Boddington. I cursed myself for having come here. Obviously Wilson's store, as being the biggest warmed space in the Wild Wood, was going to be the scene of a meeting. It didn't sound like fun to me.

Out of the corner of my eye I saw a familiar piece of pale musliny material by the sugar sacks. It was our Dolly! Forgetting my conversation with Radcliffe, I left the startled weasel holding my coat and scarf, and pushed my way through the crush.

'What's this then, Doff?' I asked her, sharply. 'Why ain't you at home with Mother and the kids? You shouldn't be gallivanting round the Wood at this time. It's nearly dark.'

She tossed her head rather pertly.

'Well I'm not gallivanting then, Cleverdick,' she told me. 'I come over for some flour that you didn't manage to bring yesterday. And then there's this meeting, so I thought I'd better stay. The Chief Weasel's to speak.'

'The Chief Weasel? Blimey, what for?'

But I seemed destined not to get any solid answers to anything that afternoon, for O.B. at that moment banged on a tea-chest and called for order. Gradually the noise died down and he began to speak.

'My friends,' he said. 'Weasels, ferrets, stoats and other—'

'Speak up,' shouted someone at the back. 'Can't hear a word!'

Another added: 'Can't see you neither, young feller. Why don't you stand on the counter?'

There was a chorus of assent, so O.B. started to clamber up. I took the opportunity to have another little go at Dolly.

'Anyway,' I said. 'You still should be at home, a young ferret of your age. Meetings aren't for kids. What'll Mother say? She'll be frantic. How were you planning to get home, all alone in the dark?'

Dolly coloured.

'Kid yourself,' she said with spirit. 'I'm nearly as old as you, anyway, Bax Ferret! And besides' – she went even redder – 'I won't be on my own. O.B. said he'd see me back to the hole.' There was a very slight pause.

'And... Mr Boddington.'

Bang bang bang bang bang went O.B.'s great polished boot on the mahogany counter. When the renewed outbreak of chatter was stilled, he took a deep breath.

'I won't bother with all the silly "Friends, animals, countrymen" stuff, if you don't mind,' he said. 'Things are too serious. As you know, my father the Chief Weasel's coming here shortly, and I've got a good idea what he's going to say. Some of you may agree with him, some of you may not. But what happened last night happened, and whatever you think about it, there was a good reason for it.'

A couple of wizened old ferrets in the far corner started jumping up and down like two-year-olds at this. One shook his fist and shouted: 'Rubbish! No reason for it at all! Young tearaways!' The other added hoarsely: 'He'm right! He'm right! Young hooligans, get us all in trouble! Should have their ears boxed.'

O.B. looked a little helpless for a moment, so Wilson banged on the counter for order.

'Listen to what he've got to say, you daft old mujjens,' he roared. 'You can 'ave your say later.'

O.B. tried again.

'Well there *was* a good reason, and that's a fact,' he said. 'Please try and hear me out, then you might change your minds. That Mole bloke should never have come here on his own, and he deserved what he got – which wasn't much, in any case. All right, so some of us chivvied him up a bit—'

A young stoat near the front shouted: 'That we did! And chased him around. Frightened him half to death, we did. Serve 'im right!'

This caused another uproar, with animals turning on each other and arguing fiercely and loudly among themselves. In general terms, it seemed to be the older ones versus the younger. Wilson was banging away on the mahogany with a big brass weight, but it was some time before O.B. could go on.

'Now, as some of you may not know, I had no part in this exercise,' he said. 'But I've had it explained to me and I'm not saying I'm against it. It didn't, in actual point of fact, do no one no harm, I'm glad to say, and it did serve to show some parties that there's some things are not to be gone into lightly. The Wild Wood's *our* place, and it's not to be turned into just another fun palace for better-off animals to go a-pleasuring in. That must be respected.'

For the first time so far, O.B. had said something that we all agreed with, young or old, stoat or squirrel. There was a chorus of approval. But O.B. just looked grim, and held up his paw for silence.

'As it happens,' he continued. 'And what is a lot more serious, is this. Mole's trip here was *not* just the casual visit of a foolish and inexperienced animal, as most people obviously think. It was part of a very well-planned expedition. And the purpose of that expedition, as far as we can tell, was very definitely against out interests.'

Well, this caused a sensation. There were shouts from all sides and complete pandemonium. I must admit I enjoyed it thoroughly, not really being a part of it, so to speak.

Old Wilson, the rat, had clambered stiffly on to the counter beside O.B. He filled his lungs and let out an earsplitting yell that was clearly a relic of his seafaring days, when he'd had to make himself heard from deck to masthead in howling gales and suchlike. It worked like a charm. He surveyed us sternly, wagging his finger like a schoolmarm.

'You foolish animals, will you just listen for a moment! How can O.B. put you in the picture of what these River Bankers is up to if you keeps jabbering like jays all the time? Just act your ages, do. I'm sick of you.' He somehow made everyone feel very silly. The silence became profound.

'Well,' continued O.B. 'The long and the short of it is this. Shortly after Mole came into the Wild Wood and got chivvied up a bit, Rat came after him. Now that in itself's nothing too peculiar. They do share an apartment and they are friends. If Mole had wandered off, I suppose it's quite natural that Rat should follow his tracks.' He paused. '*And* come armed to the eyebrows with pistols and cudgel too, although it's hardly the act of a friendly animal. But...' He paused again and looked dramatically about him. 'What is not generally known is this. One: They both ended up at Badger's place, obviously by prior arrangement. And two: This morning their friend Otter joined them there.'

There was a murmur of surprise, and a ferret cleared his throat noisily, to attract attention.

'Permission to ask a question?' (He was obviously an ex Army animal) 'How do you know all this? It's a racing cert Badger never told.' There was a subdued laugh. Badger never told nobody anything.

'Good question,' said O.B. 'And very easily answered. It just so happened that we were fortunate enough to have two of our animals in Badger's home this morning. And they heard everything.'

This also produced a murmur of surprise. As I've already said, Mr Badger was a strange enough old codger, who was not really part of the Wild Wood set-up, despite living slap-dab in the middle of it. For a start he was a solitary sort of bloke, almost a recluse. Then of course, he was big, and strong, and fierce. Truth to tell, he was more than a bit frightening to us smaller fry. Then, too, he was pretty well off, by our standards. Had extensive underground rooms and passages, didn't work anymore, and wasn't short of a bob or two, as we used to say. When he mixed at all, which wasn't often, it was with the River Bankers, not us; as being more in his class, so to speak.

O.B. continued, pleased at the way he'd at last got his audience quiet and interested.

'The hedgehog boys that live over Oak Clump; you'll know them. Dad's a road-mender. They got bogged down in the snow on their way to school. Young Billy got a bit feared, though he won't admit it in so many words, and they wound up outside Badger's door. Well, you know what kids are – more feeling than sense. You wouldn't have caught me at the same lark, but they just rang the bell and asked for breakfast.'

This caused a laugh. Us older animals would have rather starved than been so bold with Mr Badger's doorbell.

'You never can tell, as they say,' went on O.B. 'He pulled them in, kind as you like, and give them a plate of porridge apiece. I told them they were lucky to get out alive, and they just blinked. Thought I was barmy. Children, eh?!' He shook his head, and we all laughed again. O.B. then grew stern.

'Now listen, my friends. They'd hardly got their snouts nicely buried in it – and they told me particular that nice old Mr Badger let them have condensed milk, unlike nasty old ma, who makes them take salt merely – when out of a door, bright as a pair of buttons, pop Rat and Mole. Of course, porridge isn't good enough for them, condensed milk or no condensed milk. It's a pile of rashers as thick as your leg, and eggs galore, and oodles and oodles of hot, buttery toast. Oodles of it.'

A general sigh went up at this, and many an eye became dim and dreamy. There wasn't an animal in the room that couldn't see it, as vivid as could be. Although how many had ever had such a breakfast, even just one such breakfast, I couldn't hazard a guess.

O. B. jerked his mind back to the present.

'Well, there's Rat and Mole, eating like a couple of donkeys, when the doorbell rings. Billy is sent off down the passageway while the gentlemen go on filling their faces, and who should it be but their friend Otter. Oh yes, surprise surprise! If this isn't the setting for a conference, I'm a rabbit.

'Of course, when he sees all the food laid out, he wants his share, and of course, seeing as how they're only hedgehogs, and kids to boot, you can guess who has to cook it. While they're at the range with the frying pan, Otter trots out the cover story – how Mole was in trouble like, and Rat came to save him, and Otter came to see they're all right. All of which information he claims to have got from a rabbit he punched about a bit, and which was only too pleased to paint a black picture of how we'd been "hunting" friend Mole.

'But it was pretty obvious he was just saying this in front of the hedgehogs to fool us. Because when Badger came out shortly afterwards, and lunch – *lunch* I ask you; they were still eating breakfast! – was suggested, Otter made it very clear the hedgehogs must go, so that they could get down to business.'

He laughed shortly.

'Nice way he did it, too, I'm sure. He'd just got a huge plate of fried ham down him, but he told Badger that the youngsters had eaten it! So while they all got ready for another blow-out, the kids were shown out into the cold to try and find their way home again.'

At this Boddington Stoat, his face like thunder, leapt onto the counter, almost bowling O.B. over. He waved his fist and shouted: 'That's the way of it, see! That's all we are to them! Figures of fun to be lied about and sent into the snow and danger. Them youngsters was lost! Who's to say they wouldn't stay lost with just a bowl of meagre oatmeal in 'em!'

O.B. looked slightly annoyed.

'Oh come on, Boddington,' he said. 'Meagre oatmeal's a bit strong. And Badger did give them a tanner apiece, which ain't to be sniffed at.'

Boddington glowered.

'Conscience money,' he muttered. 'Ashamed to send 'em out, he should have been.'

Some wit shouted from the crowd: 'Well, their mother sent 'em first! I bet she didn't give 'em no sixpences, neither!'

Everybody fell about at this. I sniggered and dug young Dolly in the ribs, but strangely enough, she didn't get the joke; just sniffed. But when the laughter died down, Sherwood Stoat, who I hadn't known was there, put in something more serious.

He cocked his head on one side and said loudly: 'All very well this is, O.B., and don't think I'm agin you, not a bit of it. But are we meant to take the words of a couple of daft young hedgehogs as gospel? You said as how that meeting was against our interests. But if them lads got sent off then, and sounding mighty sour-grapeish if you asks me, how do we know *what* went on? May have been just like Otter said, it seems to me.'

There was a general chorus of assent, mixed with the odd cry against, from the younger animals. But Boddington, not O.B., tried to answer. He got very worked up.

'You'm blind!' he shouted (which I don't think was meant personal-like, despite old Sherwood's funny eye). 'You'm blind, and you'm stupid! Of course it's evidence. Them overfed animals have got something afoot and we should be on our guard. All the signs is there! They'm getting ready to make trouble.'

Now this seemed to be going much too far, and a general uproar broke out again. Wilson was banging away with his brass weight, while O.B. and Boddington appeared to have started a private row, the brightly dressed weasel and the drab young stoat glowering at each other up aloft for all to see.

It looked like it might be turning into a real free for all, when gradually the din began to die down. We all noticed by degrees that there was a mighty cold draught of air flowing around, and from the edge of the mêlée there came the noise of shushing. As silence fell once more, the Chief Weasel came in.

O.B.Weasel's father was a very old man, and truth to tell he weren't a particular fit one. He'd been a gay young dog in his early days, very much like his eldest son was now, and perhaps – as me ma was fond enough of saying – it was his past life that had caught up with him. Whatever it was, he shuffled into the shop creaky enough, and in the quiet that followed you could hear his old lungs rattling a bit, not to mention his teeth chattering.

He was dressed in a very long black cloak with a fur trimmed hood, and had a pair of pinchnose spectacles on. These naturally steamed right over as he came from the cold outdoors to the heat of the store, so he couldn't see a thing for a while, just stared blankly around. He had one of O.B.'s sisters with him, a grave, pleasant girl called Ethel. She pushed her way to the counter.

'Come down off there, do,' she told O.B. 'Father wants to say something and he's not to be long. He's cold and tired.' O.B. leapt lightly down and hurried across to his dad. Boddington, still glowering, climbed more heavily to the ground, with an oddly sarcastic look at his friend's retreating back. Shortly afterwards, with a little help and a couple of judiciously placed tea-chests and butter barrels, the Chief Weasel was on the counter ready to address the meeting. He waved his still-misty glasses about in front of him, smiling vaguely.

'My friends,' he said, in his cracked and rather wavering voice, 'I'm sorry to have had to ask you here on such an unfortunate occasion. As you know, something occurred in the Wild Wood last evening that does not reflect any credit at all on us animals. No, not any at all. It was, not to mince words, a disgusting display of rudeness, bad-manners, hooliganism and oafishness, directed at a harmless, reasonable, well-meaning animal.'

He paused and tried out his specs, which were still too steamy, however, to be useful.

'This animal,' he continued. 'This Mole, was, I will grant, guilty himself of the worst kind of foolishness. Even despite his lack of knowledge of us and our ways, that much is admitted. But that cannot possibly excuse those of you who were party to his harrassment. You should be ashamed of yourselves.'

The contrast was remarkable. When O.B. – himself a respected animal even in the eyes of the older generation had spoken, the two sides had heckled and clashed. But the Chief Weasel's words, so welcome to some, so unpalatable to others, were greeted in silence. You could have heard a pin drop.

He cleared his throat.

'My old acquaintance, the Badger, called upon me this afternoon,' he said. 'That in itself is an extraordinary circumstance. I will admit that in my long life I have had few formal meetings with him, even fewer informal ones. Likewise his father, whom I knew as well. Let me tell you, that this one was uniquely uncomfortable, consisting as it did of a simple statement.'

He paused again; his glasses now clear he perched them on his grey, lean nose and surveyed the room bleakly.

'A statement to the effect that if any of us Wild Wooders – he used the term, I am afraid, almost as one of odium – if any of us so much as lifted a finger in the direction of one of his friends again, it would be the worse for us. *Very much* the worse for us.

'Now, I will add only this. No one, not even so terrible an animal as Mr Badger, would normally be permitted to utter such threats in my house without protest, or unscathed. But in this case, I had no answer, or excuse. I noted his remarks, thanked him for calling, and watched him depart. That is all.'

The Chief Weasel nodded. As O.B. and Ethel, aided by Wilson, helped him down from his perch, a subdued murmuring broke out. A pathway cleared, and the cloaked figure and his daughter went into the night, the old animal coughing painfully. And somehow the heart had gone out of the meeting. Within a very short time indeed the floor was clear. The door creaked and banged without cease (Wilson had unhooked the bell) as the throng went rapidly and silently home. Hardly a 'goodnight' was exchanged. O.B. was left. And Boddington. Wilson, of course. Radcliffe, still holding my coat. And me and my little sister.

We gravitated naturally enough to the big old stove, although the store was as hot as an oven from the crowd.

Wilson magically produced water, and we watched in silence as he removed the stove's top cover and placed the blackened kettle on the glowing coke. Nobody spoke a word until it started to sing gently, and a wisp of steam rose easily from its spout.

'Well,' said Roly Poly Radcliffe, at long last. 'I reckon a cup of tea's just the thing, after that. He certainly gave us a going over, I must say.'

'He spoke a lot of sense, too, if you asks me,' I said. 'I wasn't altogether sure what had happened last night, but it seems to me he's right. What had that poor Mole fellow done to deserve it, I'd like to know?'

This perfectly reasonable statement – I thought – infuriated Boddington. He stared at me with his eyes glittering.

'Oh, that's just about typical. Just about typical. What had he done to deserve it?! Didn't you even bother to listen? That animal came here by arrangement, and there's no good'll come of it.'

I didn't like his manner of speaking at all, and I could feel myself getting hot under the collar.

'Who says by arrangement?' I asked heatedly. 'I heard O.B., and I'll say this: it didn't sound very convincing to *me*, and that's a fact.'

I turned to my friend.

'Sorry O.B.,' I said, 'but it sounded like... like a load of old rope. Sounded just like you said yourself – Mole got lost, Rat came after, and Otter came after that.'

O.B. had no chance to reply. Boddington said fiercely:

'You naive and vexing ferret, you'd believe anything anyone told you. Accident my left foot! Hasn't something already been done against us? What about that silly old mujjen

Badger being turned against his fellow Wild Wooders? Whose side is he on, eh? Not ours, that's for sure. He's a traitor!'

'Oh, come on,' said Roly Poly, good-naturedly. 'That's just daft. Why, old Badger's always been ifsy-butsy. He's never been one of us. He's a hermit, a recluse.'

'*You'm* a fool, too,' snarled the stoat. 'He's a traitor to his class. *He's* had to work, even if he's well-off now. He's letting us down. He's joined the other side. What would you know, anyway? You've never done a hand's turn.'

The steam from the kettle spout chose this moment, fortunately, to change from a trickle to a steady hissing jet.

'Tea up,' said O.B. 'Let's relax and be a mite friendlier, eh? We shouldn't be fighting amongst ourselves, it's foolish.'

'Good man,' said Wilson. 'We'll think about the rights and wrongs of it more sensible-like over a mug of the hot stuff. And remember this, young Boddington. If you'm right – and I'm willing to say I think you are – if you'm right, you'll do yourself or all of us no good at all by putting people's backs up. If there's to be a row, we'll need to stick together. So think about it.'

Boddington, who if you ask me didn't like taking advice from any quarter, being a stubborn animal, glowered but said nowt. Dolly offered to make the tea, which Wilson wouldn't hear of, although he did let her nip into the back room and bring out some sweet biscuits he'd made the day before. Soon we were sitting much more amicably round the stove, sipping and crunching.

After a while O.B. said to me, careful as it were: 'I'd have thought that after your spot of bother you'd have been with us, like, Baxter. Things are going to be fair tight in your neck of the Wood now, ain't they? Winter's shaping up to be a bad one.'

I must have looked very glum, for Dolly put her hand on mine and squeezed it.

'Oh, I don't know,' I said brightly, fooling no one. 'I expect I'll find something. I've got plenty of time to look, which I suppose is one advantage.'

No one commented on that particular piece of daft logic.

O.B. was still peering intently at me, then he spoke again, still with that same careful intonation.

'Well if, as you say, you're not with us, I suppose there's no more to be said. We'd rather hoped, of course, that you'd have wanted to join in.'

I was flummoxed.

'Join in what, though? Sorry O.B., I've been a bit tied up, so to speak. What's been going on? Join in what?'

They all looked at each other; Dolly too, which was odd. Was she in this secret that I knew nothing of?

Wilson spoke: 'You know me, young Baxter. I've been everywhere, seen everything. A sailor for more years than I care to recall. Sail, steam, you name it. Well, in all those years, in all those travels, I never saw nothing get done except if people got together. We've got to organise our selves. Make a united front. You know.'

I didn't, and my face obviously showed it.

O.B. said: 'We may be wrong, granted. It may all be a flash in the pan. But we've got to make sure we're ready if anything does break out.'

'Isn't it fun,' said Roly Poly, bouncing about in his chair. 'We're going to form an army! The weasels, ferrets and stoats are going to get up a militia! Will you come in? Do come in, Baxter, we'd love you to.'

'More than that,' said O.B. seriously. 'We need you to, Baxter. You're a very skilled and intelligent ferret. You'd be worth your weight in gold. I had hoped that you'd form your own wing. The Flying Ferrets, you could call it perhaps.'

Dolly looked at me with shining eyes.

'What do you think, Bax?' she asked, excited-like. 'Isn't it a smashing idea? If there is a disaster we'll be prepared. And anyway, we'll jolly well be able to let certain people see they can't walk all over us poorer animals just because they think they're better than us.'

Well, I can only say I was flabbergasted by all this; and confused. I didn't know if I was coming or going. All this talk of trouble, and training, and armies, on top of losing my job and all, and now my own little sister, our silly Dolly, talking like a blood-and-thunder soldier herself. The whole world had gone topsy-turvy mad.

'It seems to me,' I burst out, never being one to weigh my words much, 'that since our friend Mr Boddington Stoat came to live here, some people have gone a little soft in the head. If you foolish animals don't get your feet on the ground soon, you'll all end up in prison.

'Come, Dorothy,' I added, standing and picking my coat and scarf off the floor near Radcliffe Weasel. 'It's time you and me went home to see how our ma's getting on all alone without us. Thank Mr O.B. and Mr Boddington for their kind offer, but you won't be needing them.'

For a moment it looked as if Dolly was going to defy me. Her face went red and she began to pout in a rebellious sort of way. Then her lip quivered, and she darted over to the big coat rack and got her cloak.

'I'm surprised at you, O.B., I really am,' I went on – enjoying myself, I'm afraid, and feeling very superior. 'You heard what your poor father said, and the shame of this will pain him something fearful if he gets to hear of it. Change your mind, before it's too late.'

That good-hearted chap only laughed, completely unabashed.

'It's you who'll change your mind I expect, Baxter, me old cocksparrow,' he said gaily. 'But if the worst comes to the worst – see you on the barricades!'

Boddington was not so easily dealt with. He rose trembling to his feet, and pointed an accusing finger at me.

'You'm a traitor, Baxter Ferret, you'm nothing but a traitor. If you'm not with us you'm agin us, and you ain't got no right at all to impose your reactionary views upon your sister. Miss Ferret,' he continued grandly, to our Dolly. 'I must just say—'

But I cut him off.

'If you just say another single word, Stoat,' I said nastily. 'I'll punch your silly head. Keep your potty ideas to yourself and leave me and my family alone. You won't catch *us* joining in any games of toy soldiers. And that's that!'

Thirty seconds later we were walking home through the snow – storeless once more, except for Dolly's bag of flour. It was very cold, true; but she was sniffing just a little bit too much.

Chapter Ten
DOLLY IN TEARS

Good intentions pave the road to hell, or so they say, and for all I know it could well be true. The fact of the matter is, that it wasn't many weeks later that I was not only drilling regular with a contingent of keen young ferrets, but I had also broken my other solemn vow and was working for Mr Toad.

On the morning after the meeting at Wilson's, I started my search for work. Dolly and me had got home late, very weary, still not in the mood to talk much. Ma had got the youngsters to bed, and was herself too tired to either give Dolly a real scolding, or to want to know how I'd fared in my last day with the gaffer. I told her I'd not had time to seek a job, promised to be up with the lark, and went to bed.

The search, as I knew in my heart from the very first, was quite fruitless. I went to every farm in the district, till my feet was sore and blistered. In them days you were lucky to get a civil word from the farmer, let alone a couple of seconds of his time to put your case. But as one of them explained – the pleasantest of the lot by a long shot – it was winter, times was hard, and it was all he could do to keep the hands he had in useful labour. Or, for that matter, in their weekly wages.

When I'd walked myself to a standstill, I sat on a milestone and considered. We was a rural community purely, and if there was nothing to be had on the land, it seemed to leave nothing but going for a soldier, or just walking from house to house looking for odd jobs. I couldn't get work on roadmending, because that was in the hands of a few fellows – hedgehogs mainly – who guarded their rights very jealous like, and in any case it tended to be seasonal. Other jobs, like smithing, never had no shortage of apprentices, so I'd no chance there despite being a handy one with bellows, hammer and red hot metal, while coopering, of which there was a fair bit done down our way, I couldn't cope with, I will admit. The only other chance was glass-blowing, about which I'll say nothing at all! No, it looked like odd-jobbing.

I got up on to my feet again near frozen to the bone, and set off for the town. It was a raw day, and a fair old walk, so I stopped first at quite a big house on the edge. It was quiet, with extensive grounds, a stable and an outhouse or two. The maid was pleasant enough I'll grant, but she wouldn't let me speak to her master or mistress. Said they wasn't to be bothered on no account. Well, no point in arguing the toss, as they say.

I walked away fairly down in the mouth, but put on a brave and cheery smile when I tried the next house. I went round the back – as was the way for lowly types such as myself – and knocked politely on the door. It was opened by a big, fat red-faced woman. The cook, I'd guess.

'What do you want?' she asked, nasty as you like.

'Please ma'am,' I says, 'I was wondering if you was needing any little jobs a-doing round the house? I can turn my hand—'

Bang! She slammed the door in my face. I stood there with my mouth hanging open, daft as a rabbit. But I knew better than to knock again. Off I went, with my heart by now very low in my belly indeed.

Well, a few more little episodes like this, and it had moved from my belly right to my boots. In the next hour I was accused of being a loafer, a jailbird, a thief and (worst of all in them days) a Gypsy. I'd had dogs turned on me, a bucket of slops thrown at me, insults too numerous to mention hurled at me. Two gentlemen had threatened me with the police, and one with shooting. Another had actually disappeared into his house without a word, returning a couple of seconds later with a horsewhip. I didn't hang about to see what he had in mind to do with it.

As I wandered miserably out of the little town towards the dark smudge on the skyline that marked the Wild Wood, I saw a couple of Gypsy families huddled around their fire by the roadside. They were cutting what appeared to be clothes pegs, presumably for hawking from door to door, and for the first time in my life I felt something for them, although I'm not sure what. Did they do this by choice? I shook my head in wonderment and gave them a wave as I passed. They ignored me.

There didn't seem to be much point in going on trying, so I headed for home. Apart from anything else I was famished, having had nothing to eat or drink since a slice of dripping toast and a mug of tea at six o'clock. Mother had given me tuppence out of the lucky sock for a bite of dinner, but by the time midday came round I'd begun to believe that it might be the last money I'd ever see, so I hung on to it, foolish as that may sound.

The Wild Wood, when I finally entered it, seemed to have grown darker, bleaker, blacker than I could ever remember it. There was no animals about, no birds. Nothing edible grew, nothing but the tall, hard trees that soughed in the bitter wind, occasionally dropping great gouts of snow that crashed from high branches into what meagre undergrowth rose out of the drifts.

Of course, nothing's ever as bad as it seems, or leastways, when I got back to our hole, the noise, the laughter, the jolly activity made me a new ferret in a matter of minutes.

Christmas pudding making was in progress, which was always a glorious occasion, especially done Ma's way, with all those kids as helpers. As I walked in I was mobbed by a crowd of sticky-fingered youngsters who pulled off my coat, scarf and boots and pressed me to the kitchen fire till I almost yelled with the pain as my blood began to warm up and whizz round my veins again. Dolly thrust a steaming mug of tea into my numb hands, Mother made a red-hot sausage on a sharpened stick appear as if by magic. The noise and excitement was terrific.

By the way, I should point out that although Mother left her Christmas pudding making till late in the year – the festival was by now almost upon us – she did it two years in advance, if you get my meaning. That's to say, the pudding being made today would not be eaten this year, no, nor the next neither, but in three Christmasses from now. For she was a great believer in time, my ma. Not only was it a great healer, as she never tired of telling us, but it was good for puds, too!

It was a tradition that the small ferrets, from the bottom up, so to speak, did the donkey work, while Mother played the mastermind. And as with the brewing, it was Dolly's place, being second in line of command on the female side, as it were, to be chief helper. Now as I've already said, Dolly was a funny girl, and not perhaps the brightest learner in the world. But as I've also noted, a change was coming over her, very rapid. This year she dropped less, spoiled less, and wept less than I could ever remember. In fact I kept, to my great surprise, catching Mother and me sitting back like a lord and his lady, not doing a hand's turn, while Dolly organised the army of scuttling kids, weighed and measured the ingredients with perfect accuracy, checked on thickness and texture in the mix, and organised the bringing of the fire up to a suitable temperature under the boiler. Young Saunders, who was also a dab hand at doing the things one usually reckons girls do better than blokes, was getting the cloths ready and organizing the cutting of string into correct lengths to tie them up with.

The big sack of flour, along with the smaller ones of raisins, sugar, peel and other assorted exotic dried fruits that gave the pudding its richness and strength, were rapidly emptying. I guessed that the kids had sledged them over from Wilson's while I'd been looking for work. It reminded me of the sort of day I'd had, and I became all at once gloomy for a patch. I turned to Daisy.

'Hey, our ma,' I said, trying to be jolly. 'That's a lot of pudding mix we're getting through there. I haven't got a job yet, you know.'

She saw through me at once, giving me a friendly clout with a floury hand.

'Don't you fret yourself, Baxter,' she replied. 'If a family can't have a Christmas pud – whatever's going on in the world – then times is bad indeed. The lucky sock's not empty yet, not by a long chalk, and you'll get something soon, a bright lad like you.'

I didn't feel half so confident as Mother sounded, but her thump had left a big white mark on the side of my head, which one of the littluns noticed just then. It caused a few minutes of general hilarity and horseplay, until Dolly announced the next phase in the pudding-making process. Mother laid about her with a wooden spoon, getting the troops back to stations. I smiled to myself. It really was a job to take it all that serious, like. Impossible to believe that we wouldn't somehow see it through.

Over the next couple of weeks, however, the balance between confidence and desperation began slowly but inevitably to tip the other way. The weather had set itself for a long long freeze, as had apparently my prospects of becoming a wage-earner once more. In fact, the only times I got any fresh money at all was by clearing snow from the odd front drive after a particular heavy fall; then it was only coppers, naturally. Mother said nothing to the kids, nor did she ever berate me with it, but the food position got tighter. I often went to bed with nothing solid inside but a slice of bread and scrape, from dawn to bedtime. Just to add to the problem, the youngsters' boots were all about ready to be renewed this year, having reached the end of their cobble-able existence, even despite our elaborate system of handing down and handing down from one size to the next, year by year, regardless of the sex of the next occupant of each pair.

One bitter night as I went to my bedroom – for we were even economizing on fuel now, and the burrow had become considerable colder – I heard a noise that sounded suspiciously like sobbing coming from our Dolly's room. Ma was still downstairs, doing some darning as I recall it, so I turned the door handle and went in. True enough my sister was having a good bawl, her face buried in her pillow. I went and sat on the bed, a-patting of her head. After a short while Dolly put her arms round me, sniffing fit to bust.

'What's up then, Doff?' I said. 'Things aren't all that bad, and it's no good thing to be a-crying so close to Christmas. Littluns might hear you.'

'Oh, littluns!' she snorted. 'They don't understand anyhow, and they wouldn't mind crying, they do it all the time. But Bax, I'm worried. Ma's got nothing in the kitty, and you can't find a job and you're both so... so... so *stubborn!*' She coughed, hiccupped twice, and set herself off weeping again.

'Course I patted her again, but I wanted to know what she meant as well, like.

'How do you mean, stubborn?' I asked, when she'd calmed down somewhat. 'I don't really see what we can do about it. And we have talked. We've talked and talked and talked. *And* I've looked for work every day. Blimey, I've nearly wore out me boots looking, although I've not yet earned the price of a new pair. There's just none to be found.'

'Exactly. None to be found as any animal'll tell you. But what do you do about it? You don't talk to your friends any more, you keep away from them. But *they're* doing something about it! Why can't you join in?'

This had me flummoxed. Or I should say, maybe, that's what I pretended. For if I'm to be quite honest, I knew very well what she had in mind. The secret training.

Truth was, you see, O.B. and Boddington, along with Radcliffe, Wilson and Harrison, had got quite a little militia going by now. They did drill, and weaponry and such-like, in a little-frequented corner of the Wild Wood nearly every day. They were keeping it very dark, on account of how some of the older, more responsible animals might have viewed it. But for all Dolly said I was avoiding my friends, I was kept well informed of all that went on, one way and another.

'I don't know what you're talking about, Dolly,' I said sternly. 'And I'm pretty sure as Mother would box your ears if she heard such nonsense, in any case. You might think there's no money left, but you'll change your tune come Christmas, mark my words.'

For Mother and I had talked this out long and hard. We'd put a little by for the festive season, whatever hardships we might have to face later. Christmas in the Ferret family would be, as usual, grand and gaudy, let the new year go hang.

Dolly's scorn was withering.

'Oh Christmas, Christmas! Of course we'll have a good Christmas. Of course Ma's put something by. But don't you see, Bax, it's not enough! There's more to life than Christmas. It's no use pretending. We're in trouble.'

I was helpless.

'Come on Dolly, cheer up girl. We'll have a fine time. Pork, turkey, mince pies—'

'Don't you know anything, Baxter you fool?' (This from my little silly sister. Times were indeed changing!) 'What does that matter? Why, the carol-singers that went to Mr Mole's house last night got more than that for a few songs and being laughed at by the gentlemen. Does it stop them being hungry today?'

'What singers?' I said irritably. 'What are you on about?'

Dolly explained that the field mice across the river who went a-carolling at this time each year had tried Mole's house in the flats on the off-chance, and to their surprise found he'd returned to his long-abandoned hole, along of his friend Rat. It was damp and unlived in, but Rat had sent one of them out to buy some stores – of the very very best, money no object. They'd had salmon, and cheese, and meat paste and all sorts, as well as mulled ale in quantity. I licked my lips.

'What's up with that?' I said. 'Sounds like a laugh to me.'

'They were being laughed *at*, that's what,' said Dolly, sitting up in bed abruptly and looking fierce at me. 'They were being used. That Rat and that smug little Mole jollied them up with some food and drink, made them perform like silly monkeys, then sent them off as usual. There'll be no salmon *today* for the field mice. Just headaches from drinking while too young, and smacks from their mas and dads. And probably no supper because the larder's bare. Oh Bax, can't you see we've got to *do* something?'

I sucked my teeth. Dolly was obviously very upset, but I'm blowed if I could see what she was on about. Christmas is Christmas, after all. These little traditions make the world go round. But I didn't want to set her off crying no more, that's a fact. I opened my mouth to say something comforting, but she got there first.

'Couldn't you just go and see O.B. and B——?' She stopped awkwardly, then coughed artificial, like. 'Couldn't you just go and have a talk with him? Please, Baxter? He's dying for you to come and talk, but he's as silly and stubborn as you are. He won't come to you unless you come to him. Oh please, Bax! It's smashing fun they say, even if you're right and it's all just silly. They have lovely uniform caps and red coats, and O.B. buys them ale and cabbage soup at the Goat and Compasses. Oh do go and see, Bax!'

She was bouncing up and down like billy-oh, quite excited.

I patted her head and laughed.

'All right, all right, Doffy, I'll pop along. But only to see O.B., mind. With luck I might be able to talk him out of his silliness.'

Dolly flung her arms round my neck and gave me a smacker on the cheek.

'Oh Bax, you are a love,' she squeaked. 'You're the best brother a ferret ever had.'

She plonked herself down in the bed and jerked the blankets up around her chin, obviously nothing more to be said. I tweaked the tip of her nose, said goodnight, and slipped along to my own room. Crisis or no crisis, I slept as always like a log. In fact I was asleep far too quickly even to wonder how my little sister was so well up on not only the doings, but the ideas too, of animals I thought she knew only as my friends and acquaintances, and who in their turn I assumed knew Dolly – if indeed they'd noticed her at all – only as my gawky and ham-fisted eldest sister.

Anyway, that's how I came to train with the Wild Wood Volunteers, as O.B. rather grandly called the motley crew he'd pulled together. He didn't bother to get me to subscribe to all the nonsense some of them spouted, just pointed out it was terrific fun of a cold winter's morning, and very good exercise to boot.

The stoats, naturally enough, were the crack contingent, while the weasels and ferrets took the whole thing in a much more light-hearted way. Boddington Stoat, who I avoided as far as I possibly could, kept trying to organise what he called briefing sessions, which I heard from some animals were to do with the reasons why we trained, and how the Wild Wooders would have to 'take charge' if the manoeuvres ever came to anything. But very few animals, except stoats, ever went along, or cared. He was a fanatic, was that sour-faced animal, and as such best left to other fanatics.

For the rest of us, it was quite some time before the secret sessions became much more than a game. The only thing we paid a lot of mind to, in fact, was the secrecy. If O.B.'s old man, or some of the other respected older Wooders, had got to hear of it, I think there would have been ructions. We animals knew the great importance of keeping our mouths shut when we had to; so not a word leaked out.

It may seem strange that while I was actually involved in arms training for the unlikely event of trouble between the Wild Wood and the River Bank, I should have had anything to do with those well-off animals. But it was about this time that I had to swallow my pride, and go cap in hand to the powerful Mr Toad.

Chapter Eleven
'PUT MONEY IN THY SOCK'

Christmas, as Daisy had promised, had gone with a bang. In fact in many ways it was the wildest, gayest, loudest and most gluttonous I can remember, and I've seen a few I'm telling you.

I have visions of many animals lying in armchairs with their little legs thrust out towards blazing fires, of chestnuts roasted, presents opened, legs of pork sliced with dazzling sharp-edged knives. Of Ma's puddings flickering merrily with the pale blue flames of brandy, of stone jar after stone jar of ginger wine, raisin wine, elderberry wine, parsnip wine disappearing down legions of thirsty, furry throats. Of music – with Sherwood Stoat, almost too drunk to hold his bow, following those crazy fingers with his funny eye – of long, rambling, exciting stories of the sea, and storms, and battles, and dancing girls from Wilson the rat. I remember blurs of colour, shouts of joy and laughter, as we danced in sets, in couples, or sometimes tipsily alone. I remember mistletoe, and sweet winy kisses, romantic walks in the snow to other parties, cold turkey and ham and cheese and pickles. Most of all Mother, the centre of everything, zipping hither and thither, back and forth, from pillar to post, laughing, crying, laying about her with abandon. Christmas, as she said, was Christmas; and she knew how to celebrate it.

Afterwards, after the two days or so of solid cleaning, and dusting, and polishing, of rinsing and sweetening wine jars and pickle jars, of greasing the best knives and forks and all the thousand and one other jobs brought on by a little friendly celebration, Mother cleared the hole of the children, sent Dolly off on the long walk to Wilson's to pick up some provisions, made a big pot of tea, and plonked herself down on a stool by the kitchen fire. She pointed her spoon at the stool opposite. It was time to talk.

'Well, young Baxter, that seemed to go down all right, didn't it? I think we put on quite a show, one way and another. No one can't say Daisy Ferret don't know how to have a party.'

I grinned, squeaking my new Christmas boots. There was no need to speak. Ma wanted her say, I could tell.

'That money I just gave our Dolly to go down to Wilson's with,' she continued, after taking a long pull at her mug. 'It was the last. There's nowt in the lucky sock now, my boy. Not even a pertater.'

I laughed at the little joke. Potatoes is what we used to call holes in socks in them parts. A lucky sock with a spud in wouldn't be much use anyhow.

'Well, Baxter,' went on my mother. 'I will allow that now the dust has settled, I'm a little teeny-weeny item worried. I reckon if we'm careful, we can keep ourselves in bread for a good while, I'm not saying how long. But we've no oats for the childer, no cheese, only half a ham left over from Christmas like, and a small tub of salt. Things, my boy, could look better, I'm not denying it.'

At that she laughed, quite merry, so a drop of tea slopped on her apron.

'Seems to me,' she started again, 'that somehow or other we've got to get some money in that sock again. As the man of the hole can't find work, I suppose me and Dolly'll have to take on the job.'

I knew very well what that meant, and I didn't fancy none of it. If there's one thing I cannot abide in a burrow it's the smell of laundering, and starch, and ironing. Anyway it's hard work, low paid, and at that time was none too easy to come by. I reckon the female folk in every other hole in the Wild Wood was taking in washing that winter. Practically had to fight for the dubious privilege of washing a gentleman's dirty socks, they did. I drained my tea and got up with a squeak of leather.

'Well it seems *to me*,' I said, 'that there's a mite too many washerwomen around these parts, and I don't want none of them in my family. You just hold fire for a while, our ma, and I might be able to surprise you yet. I know I've found nothing so far, but I've another card to play and I suppose I'll have to play it.'

Mother's eyes got right inquisitive at this. She wanted to know what I was up to. But I buttoned my lip up, just smiling at her barrage of questions. I kissed her on the cheek when I'd got rigged up in my coat and muffler.

'Now don't count your chickens, Daisy,' I said. 'Nothing may come of it after all. I'll be a good while out, so don't expect me. I may come back with a job, I may not. But we don't want to see your pretty little hands dibbling in a washtub, do we, eh? Might get 'em all wrinkly!'

'Get off with you,' she laughed, waving her empty mug in·the general direction of my head. 'Pretty little hands indeed! The boy's a fool!'

It was a long, long walk to the River Bank, but my new boots were fine leather ones that felt like seven-leaguers. The air was crisp and lovely, the ground covered in hard, crunchy snow. Soon I'd worked up a good sweat and steam, and the Wild Wood was way behind me. It wasn't all that long after that I caught a far-off sight of my goal.

Toad Hall was what you might call a very imposing residence from every direction – including the river, probably, only I'd never seen it from there. It was very ancient in parts, they do say, and was all funny corners of gable-ending and long crooked ornamental chimneys. That snotty Boddington said it had only been in the family a couple of generations, after Toad's old father had made his pile somehow or other, but as you know he had a real down on Toad, on account of his throwing money about like water and his motoring. He reckoned the house shouldn't even be called Toad Hall, on account of it was a sight older and more respectable than the fat villain what lived there. His words, not mine, I would add.

Whatever the rights or wrongs of it I must say it looked nothing short of beautiful as I walked along the tree-lined driveway that morning. I couldn't guess how many rooms it had; hundreds I shouldn't be surprised. It had paddocks, vegetable gardens, water gardens, ornamental gardens, stables, a big coach-house, extensive lawns with gazebo and statues. Oh, it were a marvel. I felt about three years old and the size of a flea as I crept up to the tradesmen's door.

On it was a big notice that I'd bet my shirt said something about no hawkers or Gypsies. Nearly lost my nerve, I did, and turned and run. But I gritted my teeth. I had a right to be there, and no mistake. Apart from anything else, Toad himself had told me to come.

The tradesmen's entrance, a sort of back door leading to the kitchens only, was frightening enough, grander than the grandest I'd seen at the *front* of other houses. The bell-pull was wrought iron and had recently been black-leaded. I lugged at it gingerly, hearing a deep-toned bell jangle away inside. After what felt like ages came the pattering of feet. Well, here was something at least; the door was opened by a young weasel housemaid what I knew vaguely from the far side of Oak Bottom. I twiddled my muffler-end nervously and asked to speak to Mr Toad.

It seemed a simple enough thing to me, but I didn't know the ways of the rich too well, then. The housemaid herself – who surely should have known better – appeared to think it an outrageous sauce that such a low creature as a ferret, and a Wild Wooder to boot, should dare to want to see the master. She was all for telling me to go away herself, but after some argument agreed to call the under butler. This grand and pompous personage was at last persuaded himself. Not to seek Toad, oh no – but to summon the great, the glorious, the noble butler! By this time I was getting a bit chilled, standing on the doorstep. A bit cross too, truth to tell. But already in my first few minutes among the mighty I'd caught the picture, so I blew on my finger ends and kept a civil tongue in my head.

However much I insisted that Mr Toad had invited me, nay *instructed* me to call, the butler, when he appeared, would take no notice. Mr Toad was out, Mr Toad was indisposed, Mr Toad was unavailable for comment, Mr Toad saw no one without an appointment. I was on the verge of losing my temper and pushing this fat, morning-coated, officious, smug, infuriating domestic tyrant's snout down his throat when Mr Toad arrived on the scene.

He came, characteristically, with a hiss and a roar. There was a sudden thunder of exhaust away at the road, a hideous crashing of gears, a squealing of brakes and a crunching of gravel. A huge red motor car shot up the drive, careered across a piece of beautiful shaved lawn, dashed through an ornamental pond, and cannoned into a statue of a partly-clad lady holding aloft a flaming torch. As the vehicle came to rest the statue broke off at the knees and the lady, still smiling serenely, toppled slowly over and buried her nose in the turf. Toad had finished his morning spin.

My employment as Toad's mechanic, motor car recovery expert, wheel balancer, lamp-trimmer and general automobile adviser and dogsbody began from almost that moment. After stalling the engine when he hit the stone lady, the incompetent fellow tried to start up again to back off of her. There was a loud clattering from under the bonnet and he leapt back from the handle, terrified. I ignored the butler, who was trying to prevent me from so rudely approaching the master without filling in three sets of forms, as it were, and wandered across the grass to the stricken machine. I opened the bonnet, bent the fan blades back from out of the radiator, and started her up. Toad pushed his goggles up onto his forehead, and smiled broadly.

'I say, young fellow,' he beamed. 'That was dashed clever! I could use an animal like you! Like a job?'

'That's what I come for, sir,' I said. 'Don't you remember? I'm the farm boy, as was, that you knocked for a loop while I was driving my lorry. You crashed into me.'

'Farm boy? Lorry? I don't remember that at all. It can't have been last week, that was a steamroller. Or the week before, that was a village cross – jolly daft place to put a village cross, what, right in the middle of the square! My oh my, you should have seen it when I'd finished with it! I'll give 'em village-cross indeed! Then the week before I was in hospital, was it, or was that the week before again?'

I think he would have gone on all morning. My mouth was hanging open in amazement. But suddenly he seized my arm.

'I remember!' he cried, jumping about with excitement. 'The Throgmorton! *That's* right. There I was bowling along in the sunshine, and out you pop like a silly ass from a side street. In the town centre, too. Should have known better, my boy.'

I goggled, unable to protest or even utter a sound. Toad sailed gaily on.

'All your fault, of course, couldn't drive to save your life. Still, no harm done! You seem to know your way around underneath a bonnet, and that's all that matters! Well, speak up, boy! Do you or do you not want to come and work for Mr Toad? Generous remuneration, two square meals a day, tools and dungarees provided. Finest house in the area, if not the whole country. Make a new animal of you, working with the quality. What do you say?'

He didn't wait for an answer, nor was I capable of giving one. He clammered on, talking now to the stolid butler, who seemed completely unsurprised by all this.

'Berkeley, breakfast in ten minutes. I'll have kidneys, devilled of course, plus bacon and eggs, sausages and lashings of tea and toast. Had a hard morning's driving.' He turned back to me. 'Oh yes, and give this young fellow something, too, when he's garaged the automobile and washed her down. A margarine sandwich perhaps, or a slice of dripping toast.' He smiled broadly. 'There you are you see, young weasel. I know what you chaps like. The common touch, the common touch!'

I watched helpless as he waddled into the house, followed by the butler. Ah well, at least he hadn't thought I was a stoat, that was something. And I had a job again. With a joyous whistle I jumped into the battered motor car, found a gear somewhere in the sadly abused and sloppy gearbox, and trundled off towards the outhouses. Oh, but it was lovely, to be behind the wheel of a moving vehicle again!

After that, although the winter hardly slackened its grip, except for the odd spell, I cared nothing for it. Toad was a good enough employer, hardly one who would consciously have worked an animal all that hard, hardly one sometimes who would have noticed whether an animal was even there. He lived in a strange world of his own, in which only motor cars really existed. Whatever the weather, whatever his social engagements, he drove. He drove before breakfast, after breakfast, before lunch, after lunch. When he'd had his 'digester' as he called it, to settle his meal, he'd go for his afternoon drive 'to build up an appetite for tea'. Usually he went for a spin after tea, often for another after dinner. Where other gentlemen might take a glass of brandy or a rum punch for a nightcap, Mr Toad jumped into his car and had a last mad thunder round the quiet countryside. Fortunately for the world at large the roads were little used in them days, or the Lord alone knows what chaos and carnage he would have caused. For Mr Toad, as I believe I once pointed out to my old friend Tetley, could not drive.

That in fact, is an outrageous understatement. Put him in a driving seat and the result was a sort of backwards miracle. I say backwards because I've always imagined a miracle to be something good. I can't deny, however, that it was miraculous what he could do. Anything moving or still, small or big, was his target – or at least was there to be hit sooner or later, even if not deliberate. He often used to accuse stationary objects, objects that in fact couldn't move if they tried, of jumping out and hitting him as he went past. Trees, for example. And walls.

For us anirnals that only worked for him, it didn't matter all that much. He paid his wages prompt and regular, and very generous he was. We didn't mind the constant stream of policemen plodding up to the tradesmen's door with warnings, or reprimands, or summonses. We weren't affected, as his accountant and cashier were, by the eyestrain brought on by constant reference to the cash books as they totted up repair bills to other vehicles and property, payments to outraged or injured parties, compensation to all and sundry, or vast lump sums for the latest model. It was no skin off our nose if he spent the odd day or two in the cottage hospital. The fact that we were working for an animal who had become a household word, if not a universal laughing stock, didn't worry us at all. Why should it indeed? It was often worth a pint from a complete stranger to mention casual and quiet in a public house as how one was on the staff of Toad Hall.

But for his friends it was quite a different matter I'm afraid. Rumour had it that he was going through his inherited fortune (for Toad, as you will have gathered, didn't know the meaning of the word work) at a rate of knots. All advice was pooh-poohed – not to say poop-pooped if I may be allowed a small joke – and all attempts to persuade him towards moderation met with no response at all, except maybe half-amused contempt.

For them, the snooty River Bankers, it was not so funny to be numbered as one of his circle. Unkind remarks were common, and it was not unknown for less charitable souls to blame some of Toad's excesses on his friends. Birds of a feather, as it were. All tarred with the same brush, and so on. Whether it was due to the weather or not, it was noticeable, and much commented on, that even some of his acquaintances of very long standing indeed weren't to be seen around the big house as much as they were used to be. There was talk of 'cuttings' and 'stand-offishness' and 'leavings to stew in own juices' in the air. Even his particular chums, like Rat, say, and the Mole, and Mr Badger, didn't show up very often, and folks said as how they disapproved of the way he was carrying on something fearful.

The stories that circulated about him at this time were wild enough, but I'm afraid the reality was even wilder. Estimates as to the number of motor cars he'd wrecked ranged from about five to ten. But the fact of the matter is that in little over half a year, he'd actually been through nearer twenty, although he'd only paid for eight.

This was the way of it. In his coach-house, when I took up my employ, I found the remains and wreckage of seven motor cars. All but two of 'em – the very earliest in his line of chargers – was Armstrong Hardcastles, ranging from the Square Four

Canard de Luxe of '06, to the Single Six Camion-Cochon with supercharger brought out later that year, to their undoubted masterpiece, the Mouton Special. This had a straight-eight engine, which is to say all the eight cylinders were in a line, making the bonnet an almost unbelievable length from windscreen to the great shiny radiator grill. It also had many special features, such as its famous whirling poppets, eccentric cams, etc, that made it years ahead of its time.

To give Toad his due, once having discovered this queen among motor cars, he gave it his unstinted loyalty, to the tune of buying – and wrecking – three of them in almost as many months! My job, it quickly turned out, was to cannibalise these motor cars, as we called it, so that one or the other of them was always ready at the master's beck and call.

It might be, for example, that in his last crash the steering gear might have been damaged, and a wheel or two, say. In the crash before, or the one before that, everything at the back end – differential, axles, leaf springs etc – might have been smashed up, but the steering parts untouched. So what I did, was to take the latest casualty, remove the broken or bent steering, and replace it with the steering from the earlier 'victim' of Toad's driving. Next time round it might be a shattered engine, or gearbox. Out would come those parts from another body, and within hours the machine would be on the road again. I had a very well-equipped work shop at my disposal, with heavy chain lifts, forge, inspection pit and ramps. In fact I could well believe the master was denting his fortune, however large; for my workshop, like the Mouton Special Eight, was years in advance of what was common.

Now I'm not saying this was a good practice. In fact it was downright deadly. To be driving around in a chassis designed to take a certain engine at a certain speed on certain sized wheels, while in fact it had a bigger engine, went faster and had wheels that quite possibly came from four different models altogether, was not far short of lunacy. But then in this respect my employer was not far short of being a lunatic. And some animals would say I'm being over generous.

But whatever the rights or wrongs of it, I was working again. Hard work, and plenty of it, which I've always found makes the time fly by. I hardly noticed the days, I barely noticed the weeks, I was only dimly aware of the months. It seemed amazing when one day I found I was too hot in the morning to wear my coat for the walk to work and had to jog back to the hole to throw it into the lobby again.

My one little sadness was that I hardly ever got to drive. Oh yes, I had to take the cars to the garage from wherever Mr Toad happened to bring them to rest at night (once it took me two hours to drag one from the lily-pond), but I don't count that. The only time I used the road, the highway, the real thing, was when a new car was due for delivery and Toad was indisposed (usually at the cottage hospital with cuts and bruises, for he took the least little scrape or scratch as a serious injury) and could not fetch it himself.

It was in fact after one of these rare and glorious jaunts that the great blow fell. I lost my job again. And this time it was through no fault of my own.

Chapter Twelve
LIGHTNING STRIKES TWICE

Throughout my time at Toad Hall, I had kept up my drilling with the Wild Wood Volunteers, although I missed more parades than I got to, because of being so busy. But the times I managed to join in were real fun, especially as I now had the odd spare copper to stand my corner at the inevitable refreshment session in the Goat and Compasses after training. This nice little pub, owned by an old hare called Cecil, was tucked away in a very quiet part of the Wood, and truth to tell, he ran it less because he needed the profit, than for what little company it brought, for he enjoyed a game of dominoes or merils occasional-like.

While we marched up and down on the patch of green outside, or did manoeuvres in the trees behind, Cecil would sit on a wooden bench a-smoking his pipe and pulling at a pot of ale. Every now and again he'd go inside the little low bar parlour, through into his kitchen, and give a stir at the vast iron pan he'd have bubbling away on the range there. This was the cabbage soup, about five gallon of it. First of all O.B. had always bought it, for when the Volunteers started up it was bleakest winter and many of the lads would not have had a decent meal for as long as they could remember. And after a while, when O.B. got short of cash and asked Cecil to knock it off on account of he couldn't pay, Cecil wouldn't hear of it. From that day forward it become his treat. Funny way to run a business, I suppose, but it takes all sorts.

Not surprising, the arms we had was an assorted lot, to say the least. More guns than you might expect, but in them days many a country family had some sort of firearm, left over from the Lord alone knows what far-off time. Mainly sporting pieces, they was, some of them even flintlocks, but there was also just a smattering of ancient rifles – ex-military weapons, obviously, that some animal returning from a spell in the services had 'forgotten' to give back to the quartermaster on his discharge. Luckily for us, Harrison Ferret was one of the Volunteers, a keen one at that, and was an out-and-out wizard with guns, working as he had done for the armourer in town until the winter and slack trade had led to him being sacked. He could lay hold of a rusty, bent-barrelled, broken-stocked antique and come back two days later with it as good as new; clean, bright and slightly oiled!

If our weaponry was unusual our uniforms was worse. O.B. made it a rule that each animal had some sort of military headgear, for the sake of formality. But with the hungry and out-of-work majority, that rule had to be bent almost to breaking. One young weasel turned up on a cold morning with his ma's tea-cosy pulled snugly down over his ears, and very smart it looked too. But not only could he not hear a thing, so kept marching in a straight line while the rest of his column might left turn, or right wheel or whatever, but he got such a beating when he got back home that night that he didn't turn out again for a week; and then it was with a square of calico on his head, knotted at the four corners for all the world like a pudding cloth.

As to coats, boots and so on, well it varied. Most of the stoats very soon started turning up with red jackets, I don't know where from. There was a rumour that a few sisters, when they came to put on their best flannel petticoats for some special occasion, were going to be in for a shock, but I don't know if it wasn't just a joke. I did ask our Dolly, but she was getting too old for such banter, it seemed. She was taking life very serious these days, and unlike other young girls of her age, who delighted in whatever finery and flummery they could lay their hands to, she appeared rather to be going the other way. She didn't dress up to please or impress the fellows, but had taken to wearing greys, and dark, rather sombre clothes. A sensible girl, I was pleased to notice, for all she'd been such a flibberty-head not so long before.

To me the Volunteers was still more of a pleasantry than owt else, but I must say the general atmosphere changed as winter died, spring burst out, and gradually the summer began to take over. Cecil had started putting out big plates of cress sandwiches rather than the hot soup, and a lot of the

117

animals stayed after training to drink shandy (beer was a little heavy on those hot evenings) and have a game of bowls or a comradely sing-song. It was on such a night that O.B. brought the news that I suppose altered everything.

I hadn't been to the session, having been delayed fitting on some piece of motor car or another for the next morning, but had joined the relaxing animals afterwards.

O.B. had also been absent, I learnt, on account of his dad was ill. It was a lovely, still evening in early summer, and the sweet harmony as we sang the old songs in the leafy shade outside the inn put us all into a warm, comradely frame of mind.

> Hurrah for the scarlet and the grey,
> Helmets glittering in the sun,
> Bayonets flash like lightning,
> To the beating of a military drum;
>
> And no more I'll go a-harvesting,
> Or gathering the golden corn:
> For I've got the good King's shilling
> And we're off tomorrow morn.

As is the way when the voices are good and the company better, there was hardly a pause before the next song. Old Adnam Stoat started it, and no one minded at all that it wasn't the beginning; we could soon work round to that. His quavery, ancient voice held forth:

> Over the hills and across the Main,
> Through Flanders, Portugal and Spain.
> Queen Anne commands and we obey,
> Over the hills and far away.

But we got no further. For O.B. had come round the corner of the building. His face was very odd, a mixture of excitement and grief. Something serious had quite obviously happened. As the last straggling voices faltered into silence, O.B. Weasel came face to face with us.

'Listen, you animals,' he said simply. 'My father is dead.'

Silent pandemonium is a contradiction in terms. But it more or less sums up what we all felt then. It's like the strange thing that's said when a king dies, you know, to express sorrow at his parting and joy at the arrival on the throne of his heir. 'The King is dead; Long live the King!' For the fact was that my friend O.B., the gay dog, the life and soul of any party, the master of languages and concertinas, was now none other than the Chief Weasel.

It was Boddington Stoat who made the first move. He'd been sitting apart from the rest of us, as usual, drinking a glass of cold water while he pored over maps, or documents, or signals, or some such army-type paraphernalia. He walked over as if he'd been hypnotised, his tiny eyes blazing pinkly with excitement.

'Your father? Dead? So now you're the chief?'

O.B. nodded dumbly, still looking half dazed.

'At last,' hissed Boddington. 'At last!'

There was a murmur of amazed protest. None of us knew what to say, granted. But this was going a bit far, and no mistake.

The grey-coated stoat turned on us and glared around.

'Don't you see, you fools! O.B. is *chief*. Now at last we can move to smash the River Bank!'

We only muttered. What else could we do? Finally O.B. said, rather bleakly I thought: 'Yes. Well. Well anyway, you

119

animals. I thought you'd better know, that's all. Not much good hanging around tonight, I've a lot on my plate at present, obviously. I'll call a parade... I'll call a parade in a couple of... Well, we'll see.'

Boddington stepped right up to O.B. and seized his arm.

'But comrade,' he said fiercely. 'Hadn't we ought to talk tonight? Hadn't we better have a staff meeting now?'

O.B. shrugged Boddington's paw from his coat.

'I'll call a parade shortly,' he repeated. 'When I've got all this sorted out.'

With which he turned on his heel and strode off. We finished the cress sandwiches in virtual silence and left.

It was only a few days after this important event that I was sent to town to collect Toad's latest motor car. He was not in hospital this time, and was prepared to forego the pleasure himself purely on grounds of laziness.

Ever since he had started buying from them regular, the Armstrong Hardcastle people had had his vehicles driven to him all the way from their factory somewhere in the Midlands, thus combining the added sales compliment of personal delivery with the opportunity for their skilled engineer/ driver to road test them and complete their running in. This was especially useful in the case of Toad, whom they knew of old, as the chauffeur could point out that the car had behaved perfectly for two hundred-odd miles, in the quite likely event that he would run it into a tree ten minutes after taking delivery, and blame it on faulty steering.

The only drawback to the system was that Toad *would* insist on running the chauffeur back to the railway station in town, which had cost the company a small fortune in nerve tonic, rest cures in special nursing homes, and in one spectacular case a funeral with full hero's honours for the luckless delivery driver. For these reasons, Armstrong's had lately hit upon the idea of having their man fall mysteriously sick when he reached the town. He would send Toad a wire saying where the car had been left, breathe a sigh of relief, and jump on the next train back to the smoky environs of Birmingham or Coventry.

Such a telegram had arrived late the night before – much too late, luckily, for anything to be done about it. Toad naturally wanted to see, to touch, to stroke his new monster as soon as possible, which meant first thing in the morning. However, 'first thing' means all things to all animals. To my employer it usually had nothing to do with six o'clock. Or seven, eight, or even nine. On some days, mornings started nearer noon, or even after it. On this occasion, though, he had the incentive to rise early. So I had been instructed to walk the eight or ten miles or so to the delivery point, pick up the Mouton Special, and be back at the front entrance by no later than half past ten. On the dot!

It was a lovely morning, and I was able to rise later than usual. I wore a pair of dark breeches, and carried my lightweight chauffeur-type jacket over my arm, for although Toad let me drive on the public highways very rarely, when I did I had of course to wear some sort of livery, as befitted the dignity of the house. I wandered along the leafy ways whistling happily, not a care in the world. At the station yard the brilliant motor car awaited me. A few minutes cheerful banter with the envious railway employees, and I was on my way.

I had purposely left myself just exactly the amount of time I needed to arrive at Toad Hall on the stroke of ten thirty. Once bitten twice shy, they do say: I was not allowing myself even a hint of temptation to go for a spin on my own account.

The memory of my interview with the farm Gaffer was still much too fresh in my mind. Accordingly I swung between the imposing gate-posts and cruised slowly up the gravel driveway with seconds to spare. Almost at the steps I passed three animals who were approaching the house. From their backs I knew them immediately: The grey old Badger, the lean and eager Rat, and their stoop-shouldered friend the Mole. This was a turn-up for the books.

As the sound of the motor faded away, the front door opened and Toad appeared. His face, what you could see of it, lit up as he spotted first the motor car, then his friends. Not that you could see much, for that silly animal, the terror of the highways, was wearing his usual rig-out – big cap, goggles, leather driving coat, let the sunshine go hang. He bounced down the steps, shouting some excited greeting to them.

It was very odd. You could feel the tension in the air. It was like an approaching lightning storm. The three animals beside the car said nothing, just stared at him, their faces grim. I'm rather confused in my memory, like, as to exactly what happened next, but certainly they grabbed him, squawking like a chicken he was, and half dragged, half pushed him back into the house. Badger turned at the top of the steps and spoke to me. He told me the car wouldn't be needed, and nor would I, neither. Not today, not tomorrow, not no more. Mr Toad had changed his mind.

Changed his mind! Had it changed for him, more like! The row in the hallway was something shocking. I tried to speak to the Badger, tried to argue, like. But it was no good. He turned on his heel and disappeared, slamming the door behind him. So there I sat – jobless once more – in a brand new red motor car that wasn't mine. It flashed through my mind to drive it off, I must admit, in lieu of wages. But as I was only owed for a week, which wouldn't have bought a spoke in the Hardcastle's wheel, the idea didn't last long! I'm not sure how many minutes I sat there, getting miserabler and miserabler, but the door never opened again, nor nobody reappeared. At last I got out, flung my livery coat on the front seat, and started the slow drag home.

The carriage drive seemed never-ending. At the last curve I looked back to the house. There was the shining machine, shimmering in the morning sun. I felt a tear run down my nose, so I turned away and walked. What would happen to it I could only guess. Presumably Toad's friends would get in touch with the factory, and get them to take it away again; for like most of the wealthy, he never paid in advance.

What would happen to me I was even less sure of. But one thing I knew. I was fed up with all this. Fed up with being pushed around like a thing. Fed up with never knowing when my next wage packet might be snatched from me without so much as a by-your-leave. I was an animal too, and I wanted to be treated like one. Yes, I was an animal too. And a very, very angry one at that.

Chapter Thirteen
'VOLUNTEERS WILL WIN THE DAY'

'Now will you see some sense, you vexatious ferret? *Now* will you believe that you'm being a fool? *Now* will you do summat about it?'

It was Boddington Stoat talking, and he was talking to me.

We were sitting in the Goat and Compasses, and his nose was almost touching mine across the scrubbed wooden table. There was a mug of foaming bitter in my paw, which I had been swigging at – aye, and a few more before – vigorous as you like. He was drinking water, as usual, but he'd got fair excited on it, I must say. Dolly was sitting next to him, watching him closely, and O.B. was next to me, also supping ale. It was the night of my dismissal.

'All along we'm been telling you it's no good hobnobbing with them folks. All along we'm been thinking what a blind fool you'm been being. And now look what's happened.'

He seemed somehow or other to be quite relishing my downfall, or so I thought fuzzily. I got hot around the earholes and snapped rather than spoke.

'What's it to you, Boddington Stoat? You've been out of work for long enough. Why should you worry if I'm down now?'

O.B. let out a shout of laughter.

'Oh you are a prize and no mistake, Baxter,' he said. 'Won't you ever learn? You'd rather fight than think, you would, and that's a fact. Listen to Boddington, for once. He's talking sense. Here,' (he waved his hand to Cecil, who brought a big earthenware jug across to refill our tankards) 'empty that pot and get another down you. And learn sense.'

'Well,' I said sulkily. 'So I got the sack, all right. So what does it prove? It weren't Toad's fault this time, and no one can say it was. He was as surprised as I was, being pushed into the house like a new piano. *He* didn't give me the sack.'

'But Bax! Don't you see! You *got* the sack, that's what matters. You'd not done nothing; you were a good honest worker. And you got the sack. So what're we to do now?' It was Dolly speaking, leaning earnestly across the table. Her words gave me a sudden cold shiver. What *were* we going to do now?

'Still not Toad's fault,' I muttered stubbornly. O.B. threw up his eyes in mock disgust.

'Ah, the ferret's puddled,' he said. 'Where did you get such a daft haporth for a brother, Doll?'

Boddington wasn't so good-humoured about it, of course.

'Look, Baxter,' he said irritably. 'You was employed by Toad, and you done your work well, all right? No one had no right to dismiss you. Even Toad—'

'But Toad *didn't* dismiss me!' I screeched. 'It wasn't Toad that done it! It was his ruddy friends!'

The stoat clenched his fists beside his two ears.

'Yes yes yes yes!' he shouted back. 'His friends! That's it! If Toad didn't have no right to sack you, what right could *they* possibly have? Sheer vicious arrogance is what! What do they care? What do they care about your job? About your ma and your sisters and brothers? And your Dolly? Eh? Why should they care?'

O.B. and Dolly spoke in chorus, both leaning forward, both dead excited, like.

'He's right, Bax! He's right!'

Well, it was a queer position for me and that's for sure, to be defending the very animals that had thrown me out. Especially if you recall how mad angry I was only that very morning. Stubbornness I suppose Ma would have called it, rightly maybe. Even I could see I was on a losing wicket. I tried one more shot, for form's sake more than owt else I think.

'They only done it for what you've been saying all along,' I said. 'I mean it's like what you've been saying.'

I drew a deep breath and started again, seeing the blank looks this had produced.

'Look, you've been telling us ever since you come here, Boddington Stoat, that Toad was the villain. He's been spending like a sailor, causing danger to life and limb, and generally making a nuisance of himself. He's also become a

126

laughing stock and a bringer of insults and bad feeling to his friends.'

I paused to catch my thread and wet my whistle. Boddington, to my surprise, didn't interrupt. He was listening intent-like.

'Well,' I went on, although I'd begun to feel just how lame my argument was. 'Well, that's it, ain't it? They was fed up of him being a discredit to their names. They didn't like to see him run through his fortune like that. So they took him in hand. Drastic steps I'll grant, locking a fellow up. But that's why they done it. For his own good, like.'

I trailed off. Boddington waited for a couple of seconds, a little nasty smile playing on his thin lips.

'For his own good,' he said at last. '*Their* names was being dragged down to the gutter. *They* was getting the insults. I use your words, Baxter. So it was for *his* own good, eh? And as to his fortune. Well, I don't have to tell you who suffers when a rich man gets poor, do I? What would that velvet-jacketed little prig Mole feel like if the great nobleman went broke? How would he fancy going back to his scruffy little hole and living on cabbage stew and boiled taters again? And that layabout poety arty-crafty do-nothing Rat. No more posh evenings with his feet on the fender spouting his silly verses and smoking Toad's tobacco for *him*. No more caravan trips and parties and banquets and I don't know what. His own good, my snout! They locked Toad up for *their* own good, my friend. And if you and your family starve in the meantime, well they'll not shed many tears, will they?'

Now, when a speech like that's said quick and energetic like, you don't work too hard on seeing if it's sense or not. It sounded like sense, and despite my dislike for this grey, deadly-serious animal sitting opposite me, I couldn't for the life of me think of anything to say back. It seemed so cut and dried. I'd been thrown out of a job for no reason. I was back out of work. And Toad's friends had done it to me for what the others clearly thought were greedy, selfish motives. Probably were, too, when I come to think of it. Not above pushing Toad around, that was obvious; and as for the likes of me – I could go and starve. I didn't come right out and agree with Boddington, just dipped my tongue in my bitter beer. But they knew they'd won me over. O.B. grinned, as much as to say 'Well at last!'

'All right, all right,' I said finally. 'But what are we going to do about it? Playing at toy soldiers never got no one nowhere, did it?'

O.B. placed his mug carefully down on the table, and looked at me hard. He lowered his voice, although we were the only animals in the lonely inn.

'Are you with us now, Baxter?' he asked. 'Are you ready to team up with us and do something to get your own back on them River Bankers? I'm not talking about toy soldiers no more.'

'Oh come off it, O.B.,' I said. 'I know you. You've never taken none of Boddington's stuff that serious. You've been in it for the laugh, that's all. Are you honestly saying that that gaggle of lads with their left wheels and their tea-cosy hats is going to do something proper? What've you got in mind? Storming Toad Hall and becoming the new squire?'

I laughed at this outburst, which I considered to be quite witty. It slowly dawned on me that none of the others joined in. Boddington stared at me stonily. O.B. was drinking thoughtfully.

Dolly spoke at last.

'Baxter, don't you think you might've overlooked some thing? O.B.'s Chief Weasel now. It makes a difference, you know.'

It was a short speech, but it got home to me all the way. I thought long and hard, my head suddenly becoming much clearer, despite the amount of Cecil's beer I had swilled.

For it came to me in a rush that a weird change *had* come over my friend in the few days since his father had died. Before, it was quite true that he'd seen the militia, and the training, and Boddington Stoat's ideas, from the point of view of a diversion, something to fill his active mind. Because all the time, he'd known that his father – however sick – was the Chief Weasel. A figurehead, maybe; but in our world, the fountainhead of wisdom and strength. And even O.B. – not a particularly dutiful son, like – would never have dreamed of going against his old man on anything very important. Like the rest of us, he trusted him.

Now, however, O.B. was the leader. He'd taken over at a time when things were only a little better after a long, hard, bitter winter. A time when the rich animals of the River Bank were showing off and revelling in their superior positions in an unusually arrogant way. A time when his own best friend (for I know that's how he considered me) had been badly treated. A time when we'd seen once more how we were defenceless if someone wanted to walk roughshod over our lives.

He had taken over, what's more, at the first time in history (or at least that anyone could remember, which was the same thing to us) that an animal had suggested we could do anything about it. And while a non-thinking chap like me might reckon Boddington Stoat was after pie in the sky, was raving even, the very fact that he was an outsider who thought us Wild Wooders was soft, was challenge enough to make O.B. want to prove something. Yes, Dolly was right. O.B. was Chief Weasel now, and it did make a difference.

During my long silence no one had uttered a word. Now I'd worked it all out in my head, though, I didn't know what to say. O.B. guessed my problem, and bashed me on the shoulder, spilling my beer, the clumsy chap.

'Well, Bax my boy, still think it's toy soldiers? Still think it's just a game?'

I drew a picture with my finger-end in my puddle of spilt beer.

'But O.B.,' I said. 'What are you going to do? It's all very well talking, and all right, yes, you have got a point, sorry I laughed. But what are you going to do?'

They all started at once, Dolly as much as the other two. In the end I had to shout at them to stop.

Boddington got the first word out when they'd calmed down.

'Conscription,' he told me. 'That's the only way. All the younger stoats, weasels and ferrets will be conscripted. When we've got a big enough army—'

'Hold on, hold on,' I said loudly. 'What's this conscription when it's out? Never heard of it.'

'Oh Baxter,' said Dolly. 'It means calling up. Not volunteers anymore, a real army. We need every able-bodied animal.'

This was serious, and no mistake. But I answered with a snatch of singing. It was from one of our favourites, Over the Hills, an old recruiting song from the days of Queen Anne.

'Oh he that is forced for to go and fight,
Will never win true honour by't.
For volunteers will win the day,
Over the hills and far away!'

'Nice point, Bax,' said O.B. smiling. 'And I hope it gets into your skull, Boddington. This ferret's no fool, and neither's the bloke what wrote that song. If we try and call 'em up, we'll lose the best thing of all. They won't join us for the fun of it, and they'll likely be against us in their heart of hearts.'

'You'm talking soft! You'm talking soft!' said Boddington. 'All very well in peacetime, but it's numbers we need. And it's not fun. Try to get it between your ears that this ain't being done for fun.'

Dolly jumped in here, likely, I reckon, to take the sting of rudeness out of the stoat's words. 'Anyway, O.B.,' she declared. 'Half of 'em wouldn't join anyway, account of their mas and pas. Imagine what your pa would have said. Imagine what me and Baxter's ma Daisy's a-going to say.'

Boddington again: 'All the older ones'll be against us. Except for Wilson and a couple of them what's been about in the world. The time for messing about's done and past. Of course we need conscription. Without it... well, the stoats'd follow *me*, that I know. But could you get the weasels and the ferrets?'

With anyone less easy-going than O.B., this would have amounted to fighting talk. But that smiling animal took it easy and slow. Drunk deep of his beer before replying as pleasant as you like.

'Boddington Stoat, my dear animal,' he said, soft but with a very sharp edge indeed. 'This is the Wild Wood you're in now, if you'd be so good as to bear it in mind. The stoats might very well follow you, for all I know. But they'll follow you under *my* orders. For I am now Chief Weasel. Which means I am chief ferret as well. And chief stoat, if you get my meaning. If there's to be an army, it will be an army of volunteers. And I will be general.'

He turned to me.

'Baxter my lad, I want you to form a contingent of ferrets. I want it to be fast, deadly and efficient. I'll leave everything in your hands, but I want some action, quick. There's plenty of your lot been training, as you know. Get them together, and any more you can round up. Appoint your own officers, sergants, lance-jacks, etc. Will you do it?'

Everything was a mite blurred, but I felt splendid.

'Aye aye sir! You'll have your brigade in no time. Ah, if only I'd kept Toad's new motor car. Just think of it! Baxter's Flying Column!'

'Good man,' said O.B. 'But Captain Bax, I'd just point out one thing. "Aye aye sir" is a naval expression.'

Everyone laughed and the tension slipped away, luckily. Soon Boddington was working out the details of how he'd organize the stoats, and O.B. was deep in his pocket cashbook calculating how much of the Woodland Emergency Fund – which he now controlled as Chief Weasel – he could use to buy guns, or at least give Harrison Ferret to do up some of our more ancient and dilapidated ones. We was all very excited. Somehow or other the question of what we were actually going to do, what action we were actually going to take, didn't get raised again: it was enough that we were at last getting down to it. When battle stations sounded, we would be ready.

That important question – 'What?' – didn't worm its way into my head again until Dolly and me were walking back to the hole late that night. The air was clean and mild, with an amazing star display visible every so often as we passed through a thinner patch in the dense wood. My mind cleared gradually as we walked along, happy and quiet, arm in arm.

'Hey, Doff,' I exclaimed at last. 'Just what is it we're going to do? I mean, all that stuff about Toad and so on's fair enough, any fool can see that, even me, now. But what does old O.B. reckon to do about it?'

She didn't answer for a while; appeared to be thinking. Then she said: 'I'm not rightly sure, Bax. But something's got to be done, we all know that. Boddington says as how we've been letting 'em get away with it for far too long.'

'Oh, Boddington,' I said. 'What's he know? He don't even come from round these parts. Too big for his boots if you asks me.'

Dolly sniffed.

'Well I didn't, so there. And let me tell you, big brother, that we was the luckiest animals out when Boddie came to live here. You're just jealous, that's all.'

I would have argued, for the sake of it if nothing else, but we'd reached the door. Mother was waiting for us, and she was in a fair old mood, I can tell you. Dolly was shot off to bed in two seconds flat, with a real flea in her ear, and would have had it boxed if she hadn't been too quick off the mark for Daisy. When she'd gone, Ma turned on me.

'What do you think you're at, keeping your little sister out like that, you bad lad,' she snapped. 'I'm worried enough about her already without you giving her encouragement.' Most unfair this was, and it quite put my bad news – that I was out of a job again – to the back of my mind.

'Encouragement?' I said. 'What are you on about, Mother? I never knew she was out. I met her in the—'

I stopped. Ma would have little love for the goings on that I'd got myself into; nor Dolly too, for that matter. Dolly especial, come to think of it. It *was* queer, for a girl to go on that way. But I didn't have time to think about it then. Ma went on like a bull at a gate, very angry indeed.

'Yes, my lad,' she snorted, 'and you don't have to tell me who with. That scrawny stoat fellow, or I'm a rabbit. That Boddington. That scruffy, grey-faced little runt from across the river. Am I right or ain't I?'

I was amazed. Ma was given to outbursts, fair enough, but not like this. She seemed proper upset, as though something really dreadful was going to happen, or *had* happened, even; she was shaking with anger. All the fumes of Cecil's beer had evaporated. I was as sober as a judge. The kettle was hissing away on the hob, so I inspected the tea-pot and got down a mug.

'Well,' I said. 'I suppose you are. He was there. But then so was O. B. So was... well, so was I, come to that.'

Mother sat down, and took a mouthful of tea. She stared into the fire, looking about as gloomy as I can ever remember her. For the life of me I couldn't see what was up, so I just sat, watching her close like, and taking little sips out of my cup. I didn't have long to wait.

'You are a fool, Baxter,' she muttered. 'You've the brains of a gnat, and that's probably a compliment. You walk around in a daze. You've eyes in your head, the Lord knows, but do you use 'em? You don't see a thing. You're as daft as your father and twice as blind. I wonder you can even get about.'

Insults from Daisy were part of my life, but these was most unusual. There was no zest to them, no zing and sparkle, no accompanying clout or hurled missile. I had the unpleasant feeling that she meant every word she said. I waited in silence.

'Don't you see she's sweet on him, you daftie? Your sister, my little Dolly. She's head over heels in love with that awful little stoat. It'll be the ruination of her, you mark my words.'

I almost dropped my cup in amazement.

'Dolly!' I squeaked. 'Sweet on that bloke! Ma, you've gone bonkers! You've gone loony! Our Doff? And that...that... scrag-end of nothing! Whatever in the world gave you a daft idea like that? Whatever in the world?'

Ma smiled at me, but there was no heart in it. She looked close to tears.

'Ah, you're a good boy, Bax,' she said. 'But you're as dim as a dirty lampwick. That girl's gone on Boddington, and I don't know what to do about it. You can't help, I know, but keep an eye on her like a good boy. She's only young, and easy led. And I know something about that stoat that you don't know. He's got up a sort of private militia like, and is looking for trouble with the good folk on the River Bank. If our Doff gets mixed up in such malarkey and nonsense as that, she'll bring shame on us all. So keep an eye on her like a good boy, for the sake of your old ma, eh?'

And with that my mother got up from her chair, kissed me rather sadly goodnight, and went to bed. Leaving behind her a very confused and anxious young ferret indeed, as you can imagine!

Chapter Fourteen
THE ARREST

The next few weeks passed in such a pitch of activity and excitement, that looking back on it it still seems impossible. The days were filled with recruitment, and argufying, and even a little bit of bullying to get together my contingent. I'd get up at the crack of dawn, scoff down my breakfast, and be out of the house before you could say Jack Robinson. It sometimes only seemed like a moment later that I'd get home in the evening, pull off my britches, and roll into my bed. Time became a blur.

I got my column together by playing off the old rivalry between stoats, weasels and us. When you're young you fall for such nonsense pretty easy, so it weren't long before most of the able-bodied young ferrets was in. If they refused, or disagreed with the whole idea anyway, it wasn't many days before their special mates had ribbed them, and pulled their legs, and suggested they'd be better off with the stoats and that sort of stuff.

Then of course, there was the attraction of weaponry. What young fellow can resist the idea of getting a gun in his hand? We had Harrison as well, who although he was armourer to the whole Volunteers was under my command, being a ferret. And rows and staff meetings notwithstanding, I was sharp enough to make sure that most of the best equipment was kept in our hands. Consequently we were the crack marksmen of the whole militia – much to the fury of the stoats, who wanted to be best at everything.

O.B. boxed very clever over this one. He knew his troops would never match Boddington's for military discipline, drill and such-like, or mine for shooting and weapons handling, so – casting around in his mind for a way to keep up *his* fellows' morale – decided on the night-fighting lark. They more or less forgot rifles, except for show, like, and went in for knife training, stalking, and pistol shooting. They became experts at camouflage and invisible attack, with blacked-up faces and daggers between their teeth. After a while it quite often happened that a stoat, dressed up to the nines in scarlet coat and shining boots, would walk stiffly past a bush on the pathway – only to be challenged to 'halt or be shot' by it, and discover it was a corporal of the Weasel Brigade!

After the three basic units was formed, we had a fair number of motleys left over. This wasn't just only animals as wasn't one of the three of us, like old Wilson, who as you know was a rat, so could hardly join the Stoat Battalion. No, there was older animals who couldn't go on active service, although they were keen. Adnam Stoat, for example, who saw action during the Peninsular Wars, where he'd once actually spoken to Florence Nightingale, or so he claimed. Another old stoat, Sherwood, who couldn't shoot straight on account of his funny eye. A rather crazy old ferret called Fuller, who could still handle a sabre like a dragoon, although he wasn't quite reliable as to whether he'd run it through friend or foe.

Like all born leaders, O.B. was loath to let talent and enthusiasm go begging. He kept these often cranky oldtimers at the ready, confident that their chance would surely come. Apart from anything else, we had the constant worry – kept well in the background right enough, but we knew it was there – about what the older animals would do if all this got to be general knowledge. My ma wasn't talking only for herself when she showed she hated the idea of a militia. Ever since the night of the meeting at Wilson's, it was known that most older folk were for a quiet life, whatever the cost. O.B. might be Chief Weasel, but he couldn't count on that like his old father could, if it came to trouble. By keeping the old ones who *was* with us happy, at least we had a thin hope that some others might be persuadable.

Strange as it may seem, the bulk of animals in the Wild Wood were still completely in the dark as to what was going on. Because, as in the weird, clever, secret way that every movement of a stranger in our territory was known on the instant in every far-flung corner, the things we wanted to keep hidden, even from certain elements in the Wood itself, we could do. Only the oldest and the wisest – my ma, for instance – had an idea of it; and that only a vague one, mentioned in a moment of crisis. Having been sidetracked by that solitary mention, incidentally, from telling her of my sacking, I didn't bother afterwards. For here was the perfect cover for my continued absence every day. And while the wages I received as one of O.B.'s chiefs of staff were hardly as big as those Toad paid, coming as they did from the meagre subscriptions and anything O.B. himself could afford to add, my mother did not ask why she was given less, neither did I volunteer to tell her.

Dolly was a dedicated and active member of the force all this time. Indeed, she sometimes appeared keener and more certain of where it was all leading than any one of us.

Because she was a girl she couldn't actually be a soldier, and carry a gun and so on, which for a long time I think made her very frustrated and angry. I still looked upon her as my little sister, which was only natural when you consider we'd grown up together, but I had to learn pretty quick not to say the wrong thing, I can tell you. Very soon, if I'd try ordering her about in the casual way brothers order about sisters, especially younger ones, I'd like as not get a real bristly dressing down. If it was done in front of my friends it could be very embarrassing, and Dolly was not afraid to embarrass. She'd gone well beyond the stage of copying my ma's bluster and rant; always let you have it quiet-like, in a clear level voice. A sweet voice as well, I should add. Dolly had changed so fast I was right lost. She didn't break things no more, and she was about as silly as a naked blade. You only had to notice the way the other young fellows looked at her to see what they thought. But any poor bloke that she caught making cow-eyes at her was soon sorry he had. She could wither a lad with a look.

As for the business about her and Boddington that Mother had told me, well, it wouldn't have been natural if I hadn't tried to find out. But I could only do it by looking, after all;

the time of asking such questions was long past if I wanted to keep my ears. It's true they spent a lot of time together, but then somehow or other Dolly had sort of become one of the general staff, along of the grey-suited stoat and O.B. and me. It was done in a way that had never been talked about, and was not the customary sort of thing among us animals: she was, in fact, the only female involved in the army in any way. But she'd just always been there, it appeared, and she was useful right enough, so no one never tried to do owt about it. As for anything else between her and Boddington: if it happened I never saw it, that's all. But I always reckoned she had better taste anyway, and that Ma was up the creek on that one. For Boddington had been, was, and always would be as far as I was concerned, a big old pain in the neck.

Like I said, Dolly really wanted to be an active part of the soldiering, and although she couldn't go the whole hog, as it were, and dress as a fellow, over the weeks her clothes got even more austere in colour and cut. She didn't laugh much neither, but talked a lot with O.B. and Boddington about ways and means, and purposes, and long-term plans and strategies. Sometimes when we was walking back home of a night she'd start talking like that to me, and when I got bored with it all, or was more interested in gazing at the stars, or having a banter with the odd passing fox or squirrel, I got the feeling she was mad at me. She often used to jerk her arm out of mine and suddenly start walking fast, and stuff like that. If I tried to pull her leg about it she'd get quite standoffish.

Her main usefulness was as a sort of spy, although that's rather a nasty word for it, one way and another. What she could do that none of us could, was to find out exactly what was going on in the big house. This was on account of how she could wander in and out at will, into the kitchens, into the wash-house, into the scullery. Of course, she had to keep out of the way of the butler and his second-dickie, but with the chambermaids, and tweenies, and downstairs staff she could chatter like a schoolgirl. After all, she had known some of the domestics since they used to play hopscotch together.

She found out some right rare morsels and all. Poor old Toad was kept locked up most of the time, and his so-called friends had moved into his home to keep an eye on him. They never let him out of their sight, and one of 'em slept in the same room even, night in, night out. Sometimes there were terrible rows behind the locked doors, with crashing furniture and shouts and yells, although Dolly wasn't too ready to believe the servants' tales that their master was being beaten. It sounded to her more like he was making a nuisance of himself so that they'd give up trying. But they were a stubborn lot, and he got nowhere.

After a while, it worked out, they got fed up with all being there all the time. Truth to tell it was a lovely summer, with long, hot, dry days such as you got a lot of in them days, as I recall it. Rat was always hankering after his boat, or his swimming, or his river in general, while Badger longed to be out and about the fields and woods. Great one for walking he was, always had been. Mole, according to the servants, had become Badger's greatest friend; which was pretty amazing, considering how that grey old chap didn't bother with people much. In the end they organised a rota system. One of them would stay in all day, rain or fine, to guard Mr Toad and make sure he didn't get the chance to slip out. The other two would have the time off, to do as they liked with. Then in the evening the duty animal would be free, and one of the ones that had been out for the day would spend the evening with Toad, and sleep the night in his room. Naturally enough Badger, Rat and

Mole talked pretty freely about all this in front of the servants, for it's always the way that rich animals don't even seem to look upon their staff as human. So Dolly heard that the idea was to keep their friend under lock and key until his 'madness', as they called his fad for motor cars, had passed away.

My sister took her duties very serious, and was able to keep our finger on the pulse of events with great accuracy.

She often came back to headquarters – did I mention that we used a back room in Wilson's shop as our operations centre when we weren't on drill or manoeuvres, which we run from the Goat and Compasses? – quite excited with some titbit or other about the mad animal's goings-on. But I remember the day like it was yesterday when she brought in the news that set the invasion in motion.

It had been a lazy, heavy, muggy day. There'd been no real training activity because the thunder in the air made a lot of animals short-tempered and unpredictable, and on such days a friendly war-game with quarter-staffs and cudgels could easily get out of hand. O.B. and me had gone down to a shady pool on the edge of the Wood for a swim, while Boddington had stayed in Wilson's trying to beat himself at chess.

When we got back in the cool of the evening, Wilson was serving a young fieldmouse with a half-ounce of liquorice all-sorts. His hand slipped when he saw us coming, and the surprised youngster got nearer a quarter-pound. He squeaked loudly, but the old rat just shoved them in his paw, refused to take his money (for it needed changing) and hustled him outside. Then, to our amazement – for normally Wilson never closed – he shot the bolt, turned the sign round to read 'Gone out, back in ten minutes', and turned to us, shaking with excitement.

'Quick,' he said, grabbing us both by an arm and propelling us to the back. 'Dolly's just come in panting like a horse. Something's happened, and it's what we've been waiting for or I'm a Dutchman. She was trembling like a leaf!'

We barged into the room as Boddington and my sister bounced to their feet like they was on springs. Their faces was flushed and their eyes was burning.

'They're here,' cried Wilson unnecessarily. 'Now what's up, young Dolly! Spit it out! What's happened?'

Dolly stared at us, a look of ecstasy on her face.

'Oh, Bax,' she said. 'Oh, O.B.! Oh, Wilson! It's Toad. He's been arrested. He escaped from the Hall and stole a motor car. He drove miles and miles, as furious as a madman. Then they arrested him!'

She would have gone on, but Boddington seized her wrist and silenced her. He looked grimly at all our faces, one by one.

'Comrades,' he said at last. 'Comrades. The time has come. If you'm got any sense at all O.B., you'll call a general alert tonight. We must move at once.'

O.B. smiled quite calm-like, although I was near enough to see he was trembling. He spoke not to the imperious Boddington, but to my sister.

'Miss Ferret,' he said. 'I thank you for your valuable information. But is there anything you can add? Toad, you say, has been arrested. Do we know on what grounds? Do we know if charges have been laid? Has anything materially been altered at Toad Hall, except for the absence of the master? Is it still in the hands of his friends?'

'Hang questions, you milksop!' shouted Boddington furiously. 'We must act immediately. Strike while the iron is hot. We must invade.'

The Chief Weasel smiled, still.

'Mr Stoat,' he told Boddington. 'I am as anxious as you for action. But I will not be rushed into a rash move. The situation must be clear. Dolly,' he began again. 'Do you know anything else? Are Badger and Co still there?'

Dolly shrugged helplessly.

'I think so. Yes. All I know is Toad has been arrested.'

O.B. thought for a moment. He then addressed me and the glowering stoat.

'Gentlemen, I require you to call your troops to general alert. I will inspect in the morning, and I know everything will be in a state of the utmost readiness. But before I give the word you will do nothing else. Nothing. Is that quite clearly understood?'

I nodded, but Boddington Stoat said nowt. O.B. addressed him alone, coldly.

'Is that clearly understood, Mr Stoat?' he repeated.

There was a long silence, then Boddington muttered his assent.

It was indeed clearly understood.

Chapter Fifteen
LOVELY WEATHER FOR AN INVASION

My friend O.B., that wise general, was right of course. Despite constant and unflagging pressure from Boddington, he firmly refused to go ahead with an invasion until the confusion surrounding the arrest, and the future of Toad and his mansion, had clarified. He did not have long to wait. The antics of that foolish animal over many months, his widespread reputation as a menace and a roadhog, hardly made the law sympathetic to any merits of his case. Too conceited to brief a lawyer to plead for him, he was within a few weeks tried, convicted and sentenced. The River Bankers were flabbergasted at the severity of the sentence, but in the Wild Wood we rejoiced that at last and for once justice had been done, despite the wealth of the accused and the many strings he could no doubt have pulled if he had not been blind to everything but his own self-importance. Yes, within a few weeks the snobbish, boastful, rude, mad, profligate and exceedingly ugly animal had been put away in a dank, dark, medieval dungeon for no less than twenty years!

After that, the next move was inevitable. O.B., who'd been fighting his own nature like mad (for he dearly loved action), was bursting with excitement. Even now, however, he insisted on doing things properly. He called an immediate meeting of the general staff to discuss details. We started without Dolly, who'd been despatched to Toad Hall when the sentence was announced, to see how it had been taken by the animal's friends. Since Toad's arrest, Badger and Mole had gone on living there, to look after the place they said, despite no longer having a prisoner to guard. Rat, although he was meant to be all dreamy and a bit of a poet, had been a lot more practical and gone back to his house on the River Bank, to his boating and swimming.

We met in the back room at Wilson's, and three more excited animals it would have been impossible to find. There was a table, of course, round which we'd normally sit, but most of the time one or the other of us would jump up and dance crazily about the place. And that, believe it or not, included Boddington! On the table we'd got the maps and plans spread out, with such military essentials like cover, firing positions and areas of special danger marked in. When we'd all settled down somewhat, we got our noses stuck into 'em.

'Right, me boys,' said O.B. 'Down to business. The training's over. The games is done. What is about to commence, my friends, is the real thing!'

'Do we move tonight?' said the stoat. 'Why wait any longer? My men's bagnets is so sharp, and their brass so polished up, they'll go off pop if we don't march soon!'

'Aye,' chips in me. 'And mine's just about ready to burst! Let's do it while the vim's a-bubbling! We'm been waiting long enough!'

'Now don't jump the gun, boys, don't jump the gun,' said O.B. 'There's still a lot to be thought out. Like, for example, who's going to be there to meet us? And how many fronts is we going to attack on? And how many animals is going in on the first wave and how many on the second, and so on?'

Boddington jumped about in his chair.

'Oh blooming heck, O.B.,' he squawked. 'Don't say you'm still playing cautious. Let's just up and at 'em. Let's say to the troops: Right men, death or glory. We'm going over the top and it's every man for himself. A sea of red coats and flashing sabres! Wave after wave of daring stop-at nowts!'

I leapt off my seat and fair skipped about the room.

'That's it, that's it! Riflemen marching in threes! Rank one: Fire! They fires, then drop to their knees to reload. Rank two: Fire! They drops down, too. Rank three: Fire! Then on we goes to the next point. We'll carry all afore us, O.B. Let's just up and march! My ferrets is hopping for action!'

'Now listen, just you listen, you two daft mujjens.' O.B. stood up and planted me firmly back in my seat. 'Now look here, calm down a bit. I want you to consider one or two things.'

He paced about the room slowly, rolling a pencil between his fingers. Then he went on.

'Listen. We don't know yet what the opposition is. We don't know just how much they know about our plans. That Badger's not daft, he's Wild Wood born and bred, and I'll eat my braces if he don't have a fair old idea that there's trouble brewing. Now that's fair enough, if it was just Badger. But there's Rat, too. And there's Mole. And there's their mate Otter. And there's all their other mates as well, and relations, and such like. If we was to march straight up to the Hall, we might get blown to billioh.' He stabbed at a big coloured plan of the house and grounds with the pencil. 'See what I mean, boys? It's an easy house to defend. Dead easy. And a hard one to attack.'

That gave us pause for thought and no mistake. O.B. was right as usual. The house was surrounded by a high wall, apart from anything else. A few good men in the gatehouse and a mobile patrol round inside the grounds would make it pretty near a fortress.

'And there's another thing,' said O.B., as the door opened and my sister came in. 'What about the servants? What about the staff? Racing cert they'll stay loyal to the man what pays their wages. And there's a small army of *them*, for a kick off.'

Dolly spoke.

'I wouldn't worry overmuch about that, General,' she said, grim as you like. 'They've all been dismissed. Badger and Mole have sacked the lot of 'em!'

Well this caused an uproar, I can tell you. We crowded round and fired questions till Dolly got quite flustered. In the end she pushed us all away and explained in her own good time.

The way it was, she said, was that Badger and Mole reckoned they could save Toad a deal of money by getting rid of the staff till he come back. They was planning to live in the Hall, and guard it, and keep it aired and repaired. They was sorry, they said, for the loss of the jobs, but it wasn't to be helped. Toad had run through a lot of good cash and someone had to suffer for it.

'Sorry!' exploded Boddington, his eyes glittering with rage. 'Sorry! I should say they'm sorry, chucking innocent folks into the poor-house! Sorry! I should just about think they ought to be!'

'You should have seen them a-weeping and a-crying,' said Dolly. 'All the servant girls. All the gardeners. Why, some of 'em had been there since I don't know when. That old Vole what done the stone-masoning was born there, in a lodge, they do say.'

'We'll show 'em,' said Boddington. 'We'll show 'em. Oh, there'll be a day of reckoning, I can tell you. When we've driven the River Bankers out, them poor animals what's been made homeless shall live there again. Only this time it'll be *their* hall, not Toad's. The servants shall rule. And the poor shall come in too, and we'll all eat good meat and drink good drink!'

'Oh Boddie,' said our Doff. 'Won't it be wonderful! Brotherhood Hall, it should be called. Brotherhood Hall.'

I picked her up and swung her round the little room with a yell.

'And so it shall, Dolly, so it shall! Ain't that so, O.B.? We'll take it and open it to one and all. And rename it Brotherhood Hall!'

The Chief Weasel smiled vaguely, but he looked troubled. We all got quieter slowly.

'Listen, Dolly,' he said at last. 'Did I get you right? Did you say "until Toad got back"? Did them animals say he was coming back? Or did they mean to put the staff on a twenty year wait, like?'

Dolly went dead serious.

'Oh yes, O.B. That's what I meant to say. Badger told the staff and servants as he reckoned they wouldn't have long to wait. He reckoned no prison could hold Toad for long, and he was a rich man, anyway. Money talks, said Badger, you'll see. Toad'll be back.'

'Rubbish, rubbish,' snapped the stoat. 'It's just a sop. Just words to make the poor servants think they'm not so hard done by. Toad'll never come back. Come on, come on, let's get moving. The march must begin at once!'

O.B. seized his wrist and squeezed it till Boddington cooled off.

'Hold hard, my friend,' he said. 'We've still a few things to work out. We know the servants have gone, fair enough. But we still don't know what the strength of the garrison in Toad Hall will be.'

'You heard the girl!' said Boddington. 'Just Badger and Mole! No one else at all!'

'Oh yes,' replied O.B. coldly. 'That's *very* likely, ain't it? After they've sacked the staff? When they know something's in the air? They'd be very foolish if that was the case. At the very least they'll be armed to the teeth and as watchful as a treeful of owls. We've got to be careful.'

I honestly thought the stoat would explode. He went a dull, hot, red colour, and his teeth clacked shut.

My sister laid a paw on his arm in a comforting sort of way, and I must admit I could see his point. Everyone was keyed up with waiting, and the story of how all the servants had been made homeless and jobless would just make everyone so mad angry it would be near impossible to stop the militia boys from wanting to go straight in. But I trusted O.B. completely. I knew he wanted to invade, and I knew he wanted it to come off.

'Look, Boddington,' I said. 'I'm just as keen as you are to go in. So's O.B., I know. But it's no good if it goes off at half cock, is it? If we ups and marches there now, what'll happen? We could meet the servants coming out. Or we could find dozens of otters and badgers and other such big strong folk. It could be chaos and confusion. I don't know the right thing to do, but I reckon O.B. does. And he's the general, anyway.'

There was a long pause. Slowly everyone's breathing got more normal, like. Dolly sat down, then I did. O.B. stared hard at the big map on the table, thinking. After a while he looked at Boddington. He smiled.

'Tell you what, my friend,' he said. 'If you can keep your troops in check for just a couple more days, just a couple mind, we'll be all right.'

I jumped up.

'What's the plan, O.B.? Are we to move?'

The Chief Weasel pointed at the ground plan.

'We'll go in in three contingents; weasels, ferrets, stoats. It'll be a secret operation, not a frontal assault. It'll be carried out at night, in total silence. If we do run up against heavy odds, we'll have surprise on our side. When we get in, I don't want them even to have known we were in the same county. Any questions?'

Boddington gritted his teeth and said one word.

'When?'

'The first suitable night is when,' O.B. replied. 'I want a rotten night. A lousy night. A wet and windy night. A night when even a dog should be indoors. Until then, we've just got to keep calm. If we attack and fail, everything is lost. Everything.'

As Dolly and I walked home, she remarked that with the run of weather we'd been having, the invasion of Brotherhood Hall might *never* take place. But it wasn't many mornings later I found her sitting in the kitchen with a smile that stretched right across her face, from ear to ear.

'What's up with our Doffy?' I asked my mother.

'Blowed if I knows, young Baxter,' says Daisy. 'Little enough to smile at, I'd say. It's raining cats and dogs out.'

My sister's grin got broader. I raced to the front door and flung it open. It was magnificent. The sky was absolutely chucking it down. There was a howling wind, but you couldn't even see the tops of the trees swaying, lost as they was in a grey gloom that made the whole world a dark, dripping, exciting place.

The next few hours went by in a rush. After breakfast I got into my heaviest togs, helped Dolly's mother herself in an oilskin cape, and started the rounds of my brigade. Most of them was ready, I'll say that, having noted with the same pleasure as we had what perfect weather it was for an invasion. By evening every animal in the Wild Wood Volunteers was assembled in Wilson's store, steaming merrily in the heat from the stove that the old rat had lighted special like. There was a feeling of tension in the air; tension and anticipation. When O.B. hauled himself up onto the counter and banged for silence with his boot, silence he got, in double quick time. Me and Boddington stood below him, sternly surveying our troops.

'Lads,' said O.B. 'Tonight is the night. All our training, all our drilling and practising, all our waiting; well, this is what it was for. Tonight, in a very few minutes, we shall set out for the River Bank. We shall form up in our various brigades, under our various leaders. We shall wait till the moment is ripe. Then we shall attack. And conquer.'

There was a tumult of cheering and clapping, which died away very slowly as the Chief Weasel held up his paw. They was raring to go.

'Lads,' went on O.B. 'This is a desperate venture. We don't know how many our enemy might be. We don't know how well armed. We don't know how well prepared. We've taken every possible precaution, my two good captains and me, but we ain't in any way sure. It might be a hard fight; it might be a terrible fight; for some it might even be the last fight. This we have to risk. Whatever happens my friends, we must be sure of one thing. We are doing it for justice. We are doing it for the good of all. And we will win!'

This time O.B. had to bang with his boot for a good few minutes before he got silence. Oh it did your heart good, I can tell you, to see how keen everyone was for the fight. No doubt of it at all. Brotherhood Hall would soon be ours.

'Lads,' said our general. 'Listen to me now. We'll split into three for our briefing. Each commander knows the plan in detail. Each commander knows his part in it. When briefing's finished, in ten minutes say, we'll form up for the advance to the Hall. When we reach the River Bank there'll be no more talk, nothing. Each brigade'll take positions, then await the signal to move. Any questions?'

There were not. In fact, everyone was so eager to get going that it seemed only a moment later that I was lying full-length on the River Bank, not fifty feet from the garden entrance to Toad Hall, waiting for the runner from O.B. giving the word to attack.

It was a desperate night, and by now I was sopping and soaking to the skin. My brigade, ranged all around me in the dark, was equally wet, but kept silent as the grave, concentrating on keeping the actions of their firearms dry. We all had blacked faces, and the metalwork on our guns was painted over, so as not to give so much as a gleam. We was a secret band, I can tell you, even old Fuller, who was one of the motleys attached to my section. We'd persuaded him to leave his sabre at headquarters, and he carried instead a vast cudgel. I was praying he'd not hit any of us with it, accidental or in the heat of the battle, for despite his great age he looked fit enough for anything.

The plan was simple. The Chief Weasel's brigade, being trained to it, like, was to take the obvious way in. Foolhardy as it might sound they were going to approach from direct ahead – through the main gates and up the driveway to the front door. I must admit, however, that I was sure they could do it. For even if anyone had been actually watching, their chances of spotting the weasels was nil. Us ferrets, being reasonably secret and slinky, was to take the next most easily defended section, through the kitchen garden into the yardway at the back of the house. While the stoats, who was more of a typical army, with a fair amount of noise and easily seen from a mile off, was given the blind side of the house to deal with, where no animal in his senses would be found on a night like this – the French windows opening onto the lawn, and the conservatory and such.

As I lay there thinking, with the rain beating off my dome in a fine spray, a black patch suddenly appeared against the sky. It was the runner from the Chief. The figure crouched down beside me, water streaming from its oilskins.

'Captain Baxter?' The voice was hoarse and funny, like the runner had a sore throat.

'Yes.'

'Chief Weasel's orders, sir. You're to move off in two minutes precise and do your duty. With the Chief Weasel's compliments and the best of luck, sir.'

'Understood,' I said, grim-like. Then: 'Well lad, what are you waiting for? Get on with your business.'

The figure leaned forward unexpectedly and planted a kiss on my wet snout.

'Good luck, Bax,' it said, in a normal voice now. 'Take care, won't you?'

It was our Dolly! But before I'd had time to work out how, and ask her what she thought she was up to, risking herself in the battle, she'd disappeared into the gloom. She'd gone. Thirty seconds later the Ferret Column moved off.

I sometimes wonder, looking back, how we ever found our way in on that dreadful night. We kept our eyes burning into the dark, at any second expecting some counter attack, or a shot or flare to send the balloon up sky high. But there was no sound beyond the screaming rushing wind, no assault except for the heavy drops of rain. The worst thing we met apart from the cold was the thick doughy mud in the vegetable patches, that made crawling belly-to-the-ground most extremely unpleasant, while the worst injury sustained was when a keen youngster, anxious to keep his rifle dry, got his little finger stuck down the barrel and broke his nail.

At last we reached the back tradesmen's door, which I could remember still from the day Toad became my master. This time, though, I reached not for the bell-pull but for my little leather case of lockpicks. I selected one, tried and broke it, got out another and set to work, with my dripping band of soldiers looking on. It was all too easy, for a trained mechanic. One minute later we stood in the dark back hall, listening breathlessly. We were in!

The best laid schemes, they do say, often come a cropper when put to the test. This one certainly did. Far from meeting any resistance, we were hard put after a minute or two to meet anyone at all. O.B.'s brigade came straight down the drive and up to the door smart as you like. I let 'em in, as it happens, seeing as how I'd got there first and found nowt. Then we crept over to the conservatory side and opened up the French doors. You should have seen Boddington's face when his contingent came blundering out of the mist to find us waiting for him, and not the enemy. He jolly near had us shot before we could point out his mistake. After a short time creeping about we narrowed it down to one room. The whole house was deserted, except for one room. Inside it was the low sound of voices, with the odd laugh or two.

'What room is that, Captain Baxter?' O.B. asked me.

'The smoking-room, sir,' I whispered back. 'They'll be having a drink and a chat. Shall we go in and arrest them?'

But O.B. knew his troops. Bad enough to have met no resistance. All that training and then no fight. Something had to be done to make them feel as though they'd tasted danger. He got all the weapons stacked in a heap, then gathered the Volunteers together with as many sticks as could be mustered. They was split into three, and positioned at the three doors to the big old-fashioned room.

'Now lads,' he whispered, when all was ready. 'When I fire this pistol I want action. Break down them doors in a jiffy or quicker, and grab them dangerous animals before they can get their wits. And lads... I warn you to be quick. For the Badger is likely one of 'em. And he's a terrible fighter.'

156

There was a crack, followed by a shower of plaster as the bullet hit the ceiling. Then a whoop from all our throats and the splintering of good old oak as the doors were shattered and the Volunteers streamed in.

Badger and the Mole were sitting by a roaring log fire, their feet on stools, with long clay pipes and jugs of ale in their hands. Mole threw up his short legs in amazement and rolled his armchair right over backwards, spilling beer and sparks everywhere. Badger tried to stand, but was thrust back by dozens of eager hands. In seconds it was all over. The unlucky fellows, coatless and a little bruised, but otherwise no worse for wear, were chucked out into the cold, wet, dreary night where we'd so recently come from, to find their way home as best they might.

Brotherhood Hall was ours.

Chapter Sixteen
DOLLY DROPS A BOMBSHELL

The trouble was, I don't mind admitting it, that everyone felt terrible. I stood among that assorted band of damp, chilled, dripping animals, and I was nearly crying, honest. It was such a rotten lousy waste. All that waiting. All that planning. All that training. Then this. A bunch of kids could have taken Toad Hall, and we knew it. Such was glory. Such was might. Such was right. Any bruises and insults Badger and Mole had picked up seemed almost justified in a way. At least they might have had the grace to *look* dangerous. We'd come expecting trouble. And we'd been let down something cruel.

Dolly threw back the hood of her oilskin cloak and shook the water out of her fur.

'Baxter,' she said briskly. 'Detail some of your younger lads to come to the kitchens with me. I'll get the fires going and fill up the troops with sweet tea. That's what's needed, or I'm a rabbit. What's more we should be able to rustle up a bit of grub, even if it's only bread and cheese.'

There was a stir of interest at this sensible suggestion, and some of the troops went off with her. But the rest still stood about, steaming and dejected. O.B. looked really down in the mouth. He had his pistol in his hand and he kept looking at it, as much as to say 'Plaster! All you're good for is making holes in plaster!' It was ridiculous.

Boddington was the next to speak. And the tone of his voice came as a proper shock. I looked at his face, and sure enough, he was grinning like a loonie. He was happy, he was excited. Typical, I thought. Everyone down in the dumps, and that stoat's jolly as a clump.

'What's up with all you fools?' he shouted. 'Why'm you looking so danged dreary? We've done it! We'm in! We'm the men what took Toad Hall!'

Nobody did much more than mutter, but Boddington went on.

'Toad Hall? No lads, not any more. Don't you realize, that after all these years we've changed all that? From now on this here'll be called Brotherhood Hall. For ain't we all brothers, and ain't we took it, eh? It's ours. All the wealth, all the food and drink, all the rooms for homeless animals. All the farmlands and the good produce that the vile criminal Toad had sole benefit of, all the flour and all the bread. Ours! All ours! We'll open up the doors to everyone. Brotherhood Hall shall be the Wild Wooders's, as of ankshent right!'

He still wasn't getting far in cheering everyone up, for truth to tell he wasn't much liked, wasn't that stoat. But one or two ears did prick up at the word drink, O.B.'s among them. He took a deep breath and waggled his shoulders, like he was trying to shift off a heavy weight.

'My brave boys,' he cried, although in a pretty half-hearted sort of voice. 'Boddington Stoat is right. This here fine house is ourn now. No more shall the River Bankers lord it over us. And remember lads – under every fine house there's a fine cellar!' His voice got stronger, and the interest of our soaking troops came rushing back as well. 'What say we goes down to that there cellar, finds a couple of barrels of the best, brings 'em up here, broaches 'em, buries our snouts a bit, and becomes beneficially befuddled, not to mention boozed to our beam ends!'

There was a great roar from the company. Suddenly all was life again. Coats were dragged off and thrown in a heap, more wood was chucked on the fire, animals scurried about, looking, searching, getting their noses in everything. In very short order two big barrels had been manhandled up from the cellar and tapped. No one minded at all that the beer, stirred up from its journey to the smoking-room, was cloudy as could be. Lots of the animals stood about, still rather damp like, with mugs of hot tea in one hand to drive out the cold, and jugs of foaming ale in the other, to drive out the glooms. Mountains of bread and butter appeared, along of cheeses, hams, and jar after jar of pickled onions.

Moderation was *not* the order of the day.

Only Boddington remained aloof from all this. He kept trying to have a serious word with O.B., but O.B. was too involved, thanking the troops, having a laugh with this or that group, making sure everyone was getting his fair share of grub and beer. But the stoat finally nailed him down in a corner as he and me was going over our strategy, and how well it had carried all before it.

'Listen, O.B.,' said Boddington, miserable now the rest of us was happy, like. 'What about guards? What about sentries? We can't all be in here boozing and laughing. Brotherhood Hall's undefended. If they made a counter-attack now they'd take us sure as eggs. And in half an hour everyone'll be too puddled to fight, an'all.'

O.B. put his arm over Boddington's shoulder, very friendly.

'My dear chap, I was going to mention that,' he said with a chuckle. 'Now I don't think we'll have any trouble tonight and that's a fact. They're routed. They don't know what hit 'em. They'd never be able to get themselves a platoon up, even. But sentries we do need. And you'm the man to set 'em up. I admire your soldiery, Boddington. Your lads are the keenest, the smartest, the most military we've got. So I'm going to give them the honour of guarding Toa— Brotherhood Hall. Stoats make the best sentries, as everyone knows.'

Well, you can take it from me O.B. was laughing at the dour stoat, but he didn't take it that way. He gave a self satisfied smile, thanked the Chief Weasel prettily, and went off to get a sentry duty on the go. Lord alone knows how he persuaded anyone to get their gear on and join him in that terrible weather, but then stoats is funny, serious folk, so persuade them he did.

I would have given myself up to carousing along of the rest of 'em, for as you know I loves a pint or two. But our Dolly turned up from the kitchen just about then, and tapped me on the shoulder. She had on her cape and boots again, and was all set up for outdoors.

'Come on, Baxter boy,' she said. 'Time to get home.'

'Home?' I squeaked. 'Home! But this is it! This is Brotherhood Hall! We've just taken it over and it's ours. Everyone's staying!'

'It may be Brotherhood Hall, our Bax,' she said. 'But it certain-sure ain't Sisterhood Hall. Our ma would half kill me if I didn't come home. And I ain't walking back to the Wild Wood on my own, now am I?'

She was right, I could see. And it was the first real idea I got that Boddington's and O.B.'s grand scheme might have a flaw. For it was all very well saying the Hall belonged to everyone, but would everyone accept it, like? I was too tired and uncomfortable to give it much thought on the long, slow, miserable trudge through the howling wind and rain, but it did occur to me every now and again that some of the other animals, the older ones like my mother say, might not see it in the same light at all.

I didn't have to wait long to test out my theory. For despite the lateness of the hour when we squelched our way into the lobby, Daisy was waiting for us, and she was in a fair old stew.

She was dressed in a long white cotton nightie with a woollen shawl flung over her shoulders, like as though she'd been trying to get off to bed for some time and not been able to stay there. The kitchen fire was low and well-poked. Mother had obviously been jabbing at it morosely while she was waiting, doing more harm to it than good. She looked up as we came in from the lobby, her face all tired and sad. But she didn't say a word, which was a bad sign. Dolly and me stood in front of her, dripping onto the mat. Both feeling pretty rotten, one way and another. At long last my ma spoke.

'Well. And what do you think you two have been up to?'

I coughed, searching for something to say that didn't sound like a fairy tale, or a lie, or just plain nonsense. Didn't get very far, I must say. Ma carried on.

'Baxter Ferret, I'm almost past bothering with you. You were always a good, sensible son as any mother would be pleased to call her own. But it's beyond me, it really is, as to just what's got into you.'

I stared at the floor. Dolly put her paw on my arm.

'It's not Baxter's fault, our ma,' she said. 'He's done nothing he shouldn't be proud of. None of us have. What we've been up to tonight is for the good of all, and one day you'll thank us for it.'

Mother snorted.

'What do *you* know, miss? You're only a silly girl as is too young to be trusted anyway. Am I to be proud of my son and daughter who go gallivanting in all weathers? Am I to be proud that you can't even get home at a respectable hour, night after night? Just look at the state of you, miss. You're like a drownded rat, not a daughter of mine.'

'We ain't been gallivanting,' said Dolly evenly. 'We've been doing a deed as should have been done years ago. We've been doing something for the good of all in the Wild Wood. All. We've put an end to poverty and hunger, that's what we've been doing.'

Mother's eyes glittered dangerous-like. Some of the fire came back into her face. She spoke sharply, to me.

'What's she on about, Bax? Just what is the girl on about? Have you been up to some badness? Have you been up to some thievery or no good? Why I'll box your ears black and blue if you have. I'll beat your tails till they're...I'll...I'll...'

She half rose from her seat, looking about her. Fortunately the teapot was the only weapon within reach. She wouldn't hurl that, you could be sure.

'Ma,' I said. 'You've got to understand. What we've been doing tonight, had to be done. We've got our own back. I mean, when Toad sacked me on the spot... No, when Toad's friends... When them folks on the River Bank—'

'Sacked?' shrieked our ma. 'Sacked! You never said that, Baxter. When was that, you bad boy? Oh, can't a mother trust her son at all no more? What is the times coming to!'

'Well that's it,' I said in a rush. 'I got sacked and no one cared. We could all starve for their money. So we done it. When they put that Toad away for twenty year we done it. We've took Toad Hall and now it's ourn. It's mine and yourn, and Dolly's and O.B.'s and Boddington's and—'

'Boddington!' shouted my mother, furious with rage. 'Boddington! That mean stoat! I knew it! I knew it! It's all his doing, everything! The militia! Training! I knew it! He was trouble from the moment he came here. He ought to be in jail. He will be in jail if I know owt. The... the... the *villain*!'

'But Ma,' I said. 'Daisy, love. It wasn't just him. I mean the ideas, all right. But there's O.B., and me, and Dolly. We all—'

Mother burst into tears.

'Oh Dolly,' she sobbed. 'Oh Doff, my little girl. How could you get mixed up with such a villain as that stoat? How could you bring ruination on your mother like this?'

I was about to jump to my sister's defence, to scotch Ma's romance idea for once and for all. But I was too late. Dolly spoke up, calm and sad like, but with never a tremor.

'Ma,' she said. 'I'm sorry you don't like Boddington, for he's a good, far-sighted animal as has done more for us in the Wild Wood than you'll ever realise. He's taught us that we've

164

been done wrong by, and he's taught us to do summat about it. One day, I hope, you'll thank him.'

Ma positively hissed with anger.

'Never,' she said. 'Never, do you hear? If I ever see that animal again I'll scratch his eyes out.'

Dolly turned pale, but she still didn't waver.

'Then you'll have to scratch out mine too, Ma.' Her voice was only a whisper. 'Because I love him. And I think we'll soon be getting married.'

What an awful night. Somehow or other we all got to bed, although I doubt if much sleeping was done. In the morning there was the little ones to see to, so nothing more was said. But Daisy and Dolly exchanged not a glance. Their red rimmed eyes seemed turned inwards, like. It was all very sad.

Chapter Seventeen
O.B. STOPS THE ROT

Life in Brotherhood Hall over the next few weeks was a strange mixture. My mother's reaction to the news was not so widely shared by the other older animals in the Wild Wood as we might have expected. Toad's shameful behaviour and the long years of his boastful, selfish ways, plus the terrible sacking of his faithful staff by the Badger and company, went a long way to drawing the teeth of the more critical elements. Toad, everyone had to agree, had had it coming to him, and deserved everything he got, with brass knobs on. The success of the attack too, and the details of the routing of the fearsome Badger and his friend – which got more than a little embellished in the telling and retelling, but that's only to be expected – helped no end. There's nothing succeeds like success, they do say. Even those animals who disapproved most couldn't help but have a sneaking admiration for the victory in battle and O.B.'s brilliant generalship. But all that apart, the overall feeling was that it still wasn't right. To us it might seem only justice, and a fine thing indeed to take and share out all the things that Toad had kept from us for so long, but to our parents and others it looked like a plain act of stealing.

So the original grand plan, of opening the place up to all, of giving away or selling at cost price the produce of the home farms, of making it liberty hall to all in need, fell flat on its face. The worst of it was that even the servants, who'd been so cruelly dismissed, wouldn't come back, either as non-paying guests in the house they'd once had to slave in, nor yet as staff again, with their old jobs back and wages doubled. I say all, but of course some did, again usually the younger, more flexible spirits.

There was also the problem of females. Naturally enough, in them days, it was undreamed of for young girls to stay under the same roof as young men, unchaperoned. Even our Dolly, who considered herself engaged (despite my mother's unspoken but complete refusal to allow any such thing) could only be at the Hall during the daytime, and that in itself earned her the frosty disapproval of many folk who'd known her since a baby. All of which meant that the cooking, and washing, and cleaning and suchlike, which was female provinces in the main in the normal run of things, had to be done by the lads. And I'll be the first to allow that although we tried our

best, Brotherhood Hall, at times, looked distinctly scruffy and
dog-eared.

At first we managed to keep the troops up to a pitch of
mustard-keenness. Right from the day after we got in, we
was expecting a counter-attack, who wouldn't? So there was
constant drilling, and manoeuvres, and training exercises,
much as before. But the counter-attack never came, for what
exact reasons we couldn't be sure. Badger and Mole and Rat
could have got together a band if they'd tried, no doubt. But wait
as we might, nothing ever came of it. What little intelligence
we could gather about their movements seemed to suggest
that they weren't all that keen to chance their arm. And the
Otter affair, which O.B. turned so cleverly to our advantage,
just made the chance of them striking back more remote like.

This happened when we heard that Otter's boy had gone
missing. It was something he did pretty regular one way and
another, but this time the youngster was off for so long his
dad got worried in case something terrible had happened.
Rat and Badger and Mole joined in the worrying, not to say
the searching. In fact it was Mole and Rat that found him, a
few days later, none the worse for wear. But O.B., that crafty
animal, got it widely put about that he'd been kidnapped by
a bunch of Brotherhood Hallers. And his dad was warned in
a roundabout manner that the boy had only been let off for
kindness sake, but if Otter teamed up against us, the next time
would be a lot worse. All my-eye, naturally, but the boy was
too young or too daft to deny it and it appeared to work. A
good thing too, for Otter was a big, dangerous animal. Him
and Badger between them could do a lot of damage, and no
mistake.

Anyway, after a while it turned out that most of us weren't
in the mood to go on playing at soldiers no more. Drilling

slackened off, uniforms was discarded for something a lot more comfy, and if it hadn't been for the fact that the stoats was the sentries and guards, I wouldn't be surprised if the place hadn't been wide open to any attack. A lot of card playing went on, and swimming in the river, and drinking and storytelling.

If any of the weasels or ferrets was forced to take their turn on guard, which they were sometimes for fairness sake, they did it with bad grace, unless they had one of the rare incidents that made it all worthwhile, and gave morale a boost, and allowed stories to be made up and told in the smoking-room of a night.

These was to do with the Badger and the Mole. Far from working out anything sensible, they'd apparently just decided to watch our every move. Rat, as usual, left them to it, taking more pleasure (and rightly so) in playing about on the river all day. But the grey old Badger and his friend would wander round the boundaries, even sleeping rough at night as far as we could tell. What they were after doing we couldn't begin to imagine, but I suppose it kept them happy, and it certainly helped us keep up discipline. When they was spotted a great whoop would go up, and shots was fired sometimes (well over their heads) and stones hurled (aimed to go wide of the mark) and great flurries of insulting and witty remarks would be flung at them, along of gales of laughter. If it hadn't been for them, I don't know how we would have kept the troops at their posts.

As to myself, well, I wasn't that bothered. Strange to say, life in Brotherhood Hall was much the same to me as life in Toad Hall had been. O.B. wanted to explore the possibilities of a mobile unit to our army, in the event of any further actions being necessary, and while a lot of the usable remains of motor cars had been carted away for scrap while Toad's friends had been in charge of the house, there was still enough junk lying about in the coach-house and workshop to offer some interesting possibilities. From early morning till late at night I laboured away, with the help of a clever young stoat name of Turner, sorting out engines and steering gear enough to set about constructing a weird and wonderful motor car.

The Chief Weasel's behaviour during this time fitted in well with the gay dog I'd known and liked all my young life. In a way, I suppose, he'd been raised to a better life than most of us, what with his family not being that short of ready cash. Leastways, he took to Brotherhood Hall like a fish to water.

It wasn't long before the hurried and scrappy meals of the first few days had turned into something completely different. He'd set up a catering corps, and appointed one of the old, worldly-wise weasels – fellow called Robinson – to be chef-in-charge. Old Cecil, the hare what owned the Goat and Compasses, was persuaded to close up shop for an unspecified period, and come and be cellarman. He knew everything there was to be known about the art of keeping beer in grand condition, and because he'd gone into the trade more as a hobby like, rather than because he'd had to, also had an amazing knowledge of wines and stuff like that. Toad, it turned out, had a collection of French and German wines that were worth a fortune. So in the evenings, it weren't at all unusual for us to sit down to a fine bit of underdone steak, say, or sometimes a nice piece of salmon, or occasional-like a roast duck with all the trimmings, and to wash it down with a bottle or two (or three or four or five) of some fine vintage – as I learned to call 'em – like the '97 Chateau Visage de Poisson, or the '84 Vieilles Chaussettes, or a light Rhine wine such as Schloss Katzenjammer or Gelbe Lederhosen. Later on there'd usually be a great deal of beer drinking done with the lads, with sing-songs galore, general carousings, music playing, the lot.

Boddington, of course, never joined in these sessions, making it his habit to be outside with his troops from dusk onwards, when, he argued, attack was most likely. The truth of the matter, though, was that he had become almost crushed by the way some things had turned out. For Dolly, after the night of her disastrous row with my mother, had been in a state of weary misery, and, while she was still living at home, relations between her and Daisy were strained. Mother let her stay there all right, and said no more about the marriage idea, and got her her breakfast when the occasion arose, but I could tell by my sister's face when I asked how things had been that I should have just kept my trap shut, so to speak.

He'd had a word with me about it once, had Boddington, which left us both red at the ears and not much better off.

He'd come into the forge when Turner was off getting a bit of iron to reshape as an engine bearer. Gone straight into it, like a bull at a gate.

'Baxter,' he'd said, 'I know you don't like me, but me and your sister plans to get wed.'

I carried on bashing at a piece of glowing metal, saying not a word.

'You see,' he went on, 'it's like this. When I first come to the Wild Wood and saw how things was with you folks, I knew something had to be done. Some on you come to agree with me, gradual like. But your Dolly, right from the first, knew what I was getting at. We thinks alike. We knows there's got to be trouble before things get better.'

All above me, I must say. Still I said nowt.

'All right, Baxter,' he said tiredly. 'You'm probably right when all's said and done. I'm not good enough for her. I'll freely grant it. I've got my limitations. But with Dolly on my side, there's nothing I can't do. Honest, comrade, you've got to believe me. She's a fine girl and we'm getting married, and that's that. If this don't work, if this time's not ripe, if Brotherhood Hall should fail... There'll be a next time, you mark my words. And me and Dolly'll see it. Together.'

I spat on my metal, to test the heat, like. I felt sorry for Boddington all of a sudden. It come to me the poor chap was sincere. And in for a right hard time, to say the least of it. I shook my head and gave him a little smile.

'Well, Bodd,' I said. 'The best of luck is all I can say. But if you do marry our Dolly... it'll be over Ma's dead body.'

He came towards me, smiling shy as a girl, with his paw stretched out as if to shake mine. But Turner barged in then, and Boddington coughed instead, stared at the floor, and went out.

'Blimey,' said Turner Stoat. 'What'd you say to the boss to make 'im go like that, eh Captain Baxter, sir? 'E could eat fire raw, that one. Is 'e your mate, like?'

I acted a bit like my ma would've, I suppose. Give him a light clout behind the ear with a pair of hand-bellows, and told him to mind his own business while we got back to work.

To add to Boddington's miseries at this time, he obviously didn't like the way things was going one little scrap. We had general staff meetings regular to talk it all out, but couldn't see eye to eye no-how. You could tell him blue in the face that the soldiery would get back on form if they was needed to, you could argue till your tongue hurt that we couldn't give produce or money or rooms or jobs away if no one would take them, you could swear black was white that drinking good ale that would go off otherwise was a sensible enough thing to do. But he would keep on about brotherhood, and comradeship, and making up for all the hardship caused by 'the criminal Toad' and his friends. He appeared to think we was all meant to behave like monks or summat, but we were only doing what we always had done. Except that now we could afford it, it was happening every day and not just every Christmas!

It was plain to see, however, that it couldn't go on for ever. Something had to be done, and soon, or the whole thing would have collapsed in a heap. It was O.B. – it would have to be – who hit on the answer. And as ever O.B., with his sense of fun, sprung it on us as a great surprise.

We'd just come to the end of another boring and rather bitter staff meeting. Or so we thought. But as we was about to get up and wander off, the Chief Weasel said in a funny tone of voice: 'Oh, by the way, captains and Dolly. There's just one thing more. It near slipped my mind.'

After we'd plonked ourselves down again, O.B. looked from one to the other of us, gravely like.

'My friends,' he said. 'The time is fast approaching when we have to do something difficult, dangerous, and daring. In short, I want your comments on a plan I have thought up. The plan is this: We in Brotherhood Hall are going to spring someone from prison. That someone is our old friend – Toad.'

The effect was amazing. Boddington's jaw fell open as if on a string. Dolly let out a muffled squeak of amazement. I don't know what happened to my own face, but it was probably something of a similar sort. O.B. looked pretty pleased with the shock he'd caused.

'Yes, you did hear me right,' he went on. 'I said we'd got to get that fat and disgusting animal out of jail. And we've got to do it quick.'

Boddington rose like a ramrod and pointed an accusing finger at my friend. His voice was harsh and cracked.

'Treachery,' he gasped. 'Treachery. I knew it. All along I knew it. Treachery!'

He didn't seem to have anything to add to that, and in any case O.B. only smiled more broader.

'Finished?' he asked pleasantly. 'My my, Mr Stoat, you are a trusting animal and no mistake. What a way to talk to a comrade.'

'But O.B.,' said my sister. 'You must allow it's a shock, like. I mean... I mean, what do you *mean* by it?'

'A much more sensible approach, Miss Ferret,' replied O.B. 'I trust and hope that when you finally marry this fractious and hasty-tempered fellow you can teach him a little of your tact and good sense.'

Dolly blushed at this, while Boddington glowered all the more.

'Now,' O.B. went on, 'this is the way of it. When we took Toad's house and made it free for all, that was all very fine and dandy. Since then, however, two things has happened. And there's a mort of trouble in both of 'em. One is this: Toad is a very rich man. And I have good reason to believe that even now, a part of his wealth we know nothing of is being put to the simple end of perverting, bending, and making a mockery of justice. In short, Toad is soon going to buy his way out of prison, as predicted by his friend the Badger.'

I butted in.

'But O.B., if Toad's getting himself out, why should we do it for him?'

The Chief Weasel laughed, and told me to shut up for a minute or two.

'The second point is,' he went on, 'that our finances at Brotherhood Hall are in a very, very bad state indeed. Rocky might be a better word, my friends, as we're almost on the rocks, and that's a fact.'

'Overspending!' shouted Boddington. 'All that good money chucked after bad! Wine, and salmon, and caviare, and—'

Dolly put her finger to her lips and shushed him gently, like a kid. He went back to sulky silence.

'As you know,' said O.B., 'I'm not too well up on this money lark. But the people who keep the books say we're at the end of the rope. We need cash. Lots of cash. And we need it quick. Getting the drift are you, Baxter?' he asked, cheerful-like.

I blushed, because I wasn't getting the drift at all. But it pretty soon came clearer. O.B.'s plan was this: If we got Toad out of jail before he could bribe his own way out, he would appear to have escaped. And after the fuss and hoohah that would cause, the wicked animal would be hurled back into his dungeon once more, with no chance of ever bribing no one again. So in fact, by getting him out and handing him over to the law again, as if we'd captured him, we'd make sure he'd be there for the full twenty years.

'It also means,' added O. B., 'that we do ourselves a bit of good. For the capture of such a dangerous criminal would make the police very grateful to us, no doubt. Let alone the question of any reward we might collect. With me?'

Even our scowling stoat had pricked up his ears. But Dolly looked puzzled.

'I don't quite get the second part, though, O.B. Surely the reward wouldn't be enough? Not if the Hall's so deep in trouble?'

'No indeed,' said O.B. 'You're as smart as ever, Dolly. But as sure as eggs is eggs, that lazy Toad has a good deal more cash than *we've* been able to find. Somewhere, either on the premises or in a vault, he must have a fortune hidden. When we've got him out of jail he'll be able to tell us where it is.'

I giggled.

'Perhaps he won't be inclined to,' I said. 'Then what do we do?'

O.B. gave a short laugh.

'There are ways and means, Bax, my boy. I think Toadie will be only too pleased to do a deal with us, one way and another. And if he doesn't care to... Well. I don't think that cowardly animal would take too much persuading, do you? Anyone want to say anything?'

Boddington spoke, a little sullen-like.

'I still think if we'd been more careful and less Toadlike in our ways we wouldn't need more money. We'm spending far too much of it, and that's a fact. Seems to me there's another reason for this malarkey. And that's sheer devilment. Are you prepared to say you'm still as firm behind our ideas of equality and brotherhood for all as you was when we started, O.B. Weasel?'

O.B. clicked his tongue and shook his head.

'Oh Boddie, Boddie, you are a disbelieving animal and no mistake. Look man, it's straight up and down like I said. I don't understand money, but Wilson and a couple of others does. We've been giving it away like water, paying tradesmen's bills right and left, and selling our farm produce at less than it costs to grow it. Say what you like, that means we're going broke. See? As to the other, well, you knows the evil ways of the rich better than anyone. Toad'll be out in a month given his head. There's no jury, judge, policeman or jailer as can't be bribed. And once he's out and free, why, he'll have the law on us as soon as blink. Devilment indeed! Blooming heck, man, what do you take me for?'

An impressive speech, what shut up the stoat all right. But as O.B. finished it he looked straight at me, and I'm danged if he didn't wink. Or perhaps he'd got a spot of dust in his eye, I don't know.

'If it's as serious as you say,' said our Dolly. 'And I'm not saying it ain't, O.B. But if it is, hadn't we better get a move on? I mean, if we're to spring old Toad before he springs himself?'

'Excellent girl,' replied the weasel. 'I called this meeting exactly because it is so urgent. And I'm glad you realise it better than our friends here, because *you're* going to have to do most of the work. For a start-off, at least.'

Dolly looked pleased. Boddington and me pinned back our ears as O.B. started detailing his plan.

It was worth a listen, I can tell you, a real O.B. humdinger.

His eyes gleamed as he went through it point by point, and he was flushed and happy with excitement. I guessed that the wink had been no speck of dust at all; the stoat was surely right in spotting a little devilment in the chief. He was bored and fed up. He wanted some action and this way he'd get it. But the blood raced in my veins as well – I wasn't complaining. Even Boddington cheered up, and his hand kept reaching for his pistol butt, sticking out of his polished leather belt.

'Well, Dolly,' said O.B. at last. 'Think you can do it all right? It won't be easy.'

My sister stood up, and saluted.

'O.B., sir,' she said. 'You can count on me.'

She turned to the stoat beside her.

'Oh Boddie,' she exclaimed. 'Isn't it smashing!'

Chapter Eighteen
BAXTER'S FLYING COLUMN

If our Dolly hadn't been so sadly taken from us, I reckon she could have made her living as a spy. The Mata Hari of the animal world, maybe. She started working out her strategy that very evening, and by next day had an idea, in rough, of how she'd go about it.

The enormous old fortress that served as a prison for the whole wide area was a good few miles away, so me and Turner worked throughout the night to get our mechanical marvel ready for the trip. We really needed a lot more time, but needs must when the devil drives, as they say. When we brought it out of the coach-house-cum-workshop next morning into the light of day for the first time, it was in a pretty dicey state. I mean the wheels turned all right, and the steering worked, after a fashion, and the engine could be relied on – almost – to keep chugging away. But frankly, neither of us was willing to put good money on how long this state of affairs would last.

My sister took one look at it and shrieked with laughter, in which I joined hearty enough. Turner, being a stoat, didn't think it so funny.

'Billy Bingo, Bax,' said Doff. 'Where did you find that old heap? What's it called, eh?'

'It's an A.S.P.,' I told her, serious like. 'One day I'll flood the world with them, and make all our fortunes.'

'No, not really?' she said. 'Is that truly a make of motor car, an A.S.P? I thought you'd made it out of cocoa tins.'

'My own design,' I laughed. 'Built in the well-appointed workshops of Brotherhood Hall by Baxter and Turner. A.S.P. equals All Spare Parts, get it?'

Anyway, the old wreck got us there all right, so it didn't matter what we looked like. But I must admit we got a lot more stares on the way than even an ordinary lorry or motor car attracted in them days.

Over the next few weeks, we took Dolly to the town near where the prison was any number of times. We'd drop her off, then hang about at a loose end all day. It was a pity, because away from our tools and our garage, we couldn't get on with the vital business of improving and testing, that would have made our machine reliable and properly roadworthy. It was to cost us dear, as things turned out. Very dear.

What she was doing, I wasn't entirely in the know about. Given such a big job all on her own, my sister took it very serious, and didn't much want to talk about it until she was sure she was getting somewhere. But it wasn't that long before a staff meeting was called, in which she was to give a detailed progress report. On the day, I left Turner tinkering, scrubbed my hands with the bar of green carbolic to get the grease off, got out of my overalls, and went into the big study where we always met. The others was already there.

'Righto then,' said O.B., when I'd parked myself down. 'We all know why we're here. Go ahead when you're ready, Miss Ferret.'

'Gentlemen,' our Dolly started, grave and formal as you'd wish. 'It can be done.' She paused. 'It could not be done, I think, with any other animal but the conceited, foolish, and boastful Toad. But with him, it will be just possible. If things go well, I think we can have him out of there and in our hands by Friday.'

See what I mean? My little sister had penetrated one of the greatest, vilest, strongest prisons in the land, and within hardly no time at all was confident of effecting the escape of its most notorious inmate. We all congratulated her, patted her on the back, etcetera. For me it was a proud moment, I can tell you. She waved her hand for silence.

'Don't thank me too hard just yet,' she went on. 'There are problems. Mainly there is the problem of cost. We can get Toad out, I'm sure of it. But it will cost us. It'll cost us a fair old lump of money.'

Boddington and me were crestfallen, but O.B., surprising enough, just smiled.

'Dolly, you're a marvel,' he said. 'Boddington's a lucky stoat, a lucky stoat indeed. But I wasn't born yesterday neither, believe it or not. I can plan ahead with the best of 'em. And despite the general low finances here at B.H., there's enough in the special safe to spring Toadie, or I'm a donkey. Aye, and to have a banquet to celebrate it when it's done!'

What had happened was this. Dolly – being a girl, and crafty to boot – had been able to hang about the prison without causing overmuch suspicion, even asking questions of the guards and warders when she got the chance. After some time, she'd learned that the jailer in charge of Toad had a young daughter; about her age, in fact. After even more time and wangling, she'd not only got to meet this girl, but they'd come to be friends, like. She'd laid it on that she was on Toad's side – vowing the girl to not breathe a word of it even to that animal, on account of his big mouth – and working on behalf of other friends, who wanted to see him free. This, of course, come as no surprise at all to the jailer's daughter, because she and her father had only been puzzled why it had taken so long, with him being so rich and that. Knowing Toad, it come as no surprise, neither, that his 'friends' didn't trust him to know the real details of his own escape – for he'd certain-sure have ruinated it!

Well, between them, my sister and the girl had worked out a plan that sounded at first so madcap you'd hardly credit it – but madcap or not, the first part had actually been in operation for some good time. This involved the jailer's daughter making up to Toad, like, and feeding him titbits and good food. There was two reasons behind it: to get him into a conceited enough frame of mind to think he could pull off an escape – because he'd not unnaturally fallen pretty melancholy, faced with twenty years in that hole – and to get him to think the girl was his friend, and was prepared to help him. Poor old Toad, gullible as ever, had swallowed the bait, hook, line and sinker. Only this week Dolly had been told he was ready for the clincher.

And this was it. The girl was going to tell Toad – if Dolly gave her the go-ahead on the money side, which would be steep – that her auntie was the prison washerwoman. All silliness of course, for what prison doesn't have its own laundry? That very Friday, she'd say, her auntie would come into Toad's cell, and for a reasonable bribe (yes, poor Toad was going to have to help pay for *us* to spring him!) she would let him have her clothes, shawl and bonnet. Then all Toad had to do was walk out like her auntie normally would, and Bob's your uncle! Dolly's idea in the main, including the masterstroke: they'd tell Toad to tie up the washerwoman (my sister, that is, with her petticoats well stuffed with cushions to fool the silly animal) so as she could say she'd been attacked, and thus keep her job; the final touch of authenticity that he'd not be able to resist.

When she'd finished her tale, Dolly looked from one to the other of us, expectant like. O.B. shook his head slowly from side to side, then gave a low whistle.

'Miss Ferret,' he said. 'Dolly, my love. You are a genius. I'll say this: I couldn't have thought up a better plan myself.'

Boddington didn't appear so sure, and truth to tell I wasn't, neither.

He only muttered 'Sounds a bit far-fetched to me, begging you pardon, Dorothy. Will it work, like? That's the thing.'

Dolly was obviously very hurt by this criticism, but O.B. leapt in to her defence.

'Oh you fretful fellow, don't be such a down-in-the-mouth,' he cried. 'Of course it'll work. It's Toadie we'm talking about remember? That bloke's so full of himself he'd believe any rubbish. He'll be so carried away by the excitement of tying up the washerwoman, and his own cleverness at escaping, that it'll go like a dream. Imagine him walking past all those warders, thinking himself to be a brave and clever master of escape and disguise, fooling them all, when all the time they'll be breaking their necks trying to keep a straight face, and planning what they'll spend their share of the bribe money on! What do you think, Baxter? Isn't your sister a wonder? An absolute wonder!'

He popped out of his seat like on elastic, nipped round the table, and planted a kiss right on her lips. As we all goggled at each other, he roared with laughter.

'Now, Miss Ferret,' he carried on, as if nowt had happened. 'How much will it cost, and how do we pay?'

'Ah well, that's it, see,' said our Doff, when she'd collected herself together. 'Even with the few sovereigns we'll sting Toad for, it's a bit dear. We've the jailer to pay the biggest lump to, then his daughter, although she only gets a small cut, in the way of things. Then there's the warders on each door, the turnkeys ditto, and the guardroom, including the master-at-arms who gets quite a big chunk on account of him being the one what carries the can in the event of an escape. Then there's the emergency fund for anyone else who happens to see what's going on, puts two and two together, and has to be shushed. I takes the money with me and gives it to the girl, who gives it to her dad, who shares it out neat and decent, like.'

All in all it sounded like a fair old whack, but O.B. never stopped smiling. That far-seeing general had obviously got it well within hand. When my sister named the figure he just nodded, muttering 'Very good, very good,' as if it was a mere nothing.

'Right,' he said at last. 'Today's Tuesday. Baxter, you get your Dolly out to the jail tomorrow, let her give the girl the go-ahead – and the money come to that – and on Friday, all being well, Toadie will be ours. One thing, Dolly,' he added.

'Are you sure Toad will fall for it? We won't just give the girl our money and him funk it? Is she to be trusted?'

'I'm sure of it,' my sister said. 'She's been working on him and she reckons he'll be putty in her hands, given the right sort of flattery. If you've got the vehicle waiting at dusk on Friday, he'll waddle straight out of the main gate into your arms.'

'Good,' said O.B. He turned to me. 'You know what this means don't you, Bax boy? Your Flying Column's going to be used at last. It'll be up to you to be there, to fetch Mrs Washerwoman Toad, and whip him back here in a jiffy. Choose your men and choose them well. Nothing can be allowed to go wrong. If Toad was to get away I don't know what would happen. He's rich, powerful, and influential. We've got to get him here double quick or we'll be in for such a disaster as I can't think. Any questions?'

Next day I delivered Dolly, with her little sack of gold sovereigns, waited for an hour or three, then drove her back. Everything had gone beautiful. She was cockahoop. The jailer's daughter knew her part to perfection.

The only change in plan was that they'd decided between them it would be safer and easier if my sister spent the night at the prison on Thursday, in the girl's room, so that there'd be less chance of her being caught out, before the jail break, wandering around as the 'fat auntie' or washlady. This meant going back to the Wild Wood, explaining to Mother that she would be spending tomorrow night with a friend, getting together clothes, and so on and so forth. On the Thursday, which I'd planned to have free, I therefore had to go all the way back to the jail to drop Dolly yet again. Precious hours Turner and me had set aside to check over the A.S.P. and iron out some troubles what had been giving us cause for worry, had to be forgotten. Apart from owt else, I had to choose the three or four lads who was to be my 'Flying Column'.

O. B. couldn't be included, of course, being the chief. He had to stay at Brotherhood Hall in case anything happened that called for a lightning change of plan. Boddington seemed keen enough but I didn't want him, which I could cover with the readymade excuse that as chief of the stoats he couldn't be spared on account of emergencies coming up. Harrison Ferret I did want, grumpy as he was, because he didn't talk much, knew all about guns (though God forbid we'd need such knowledge), and was very sober and reliable. Radcliffe Weasel, the dancer, I wanted because I liked him, and truth to tell he made me feel confident, being a jolly, good-natured sort of bloke who'd laugh in the face of all manner of troubles. The fourth, although there wasn't a lot of room for him, considering we'd have Toad to squeeze in as well, was Turner Stoat. Him I had to have, in case our neglected and overworked vehicle should take it into its head to pack up on us. Anyway he was very strong, so if Toad was in a mind to try and fight he might come in useful.

We spent Friday morning going over the details, had a light but nourishing lunch with only a pint of strong ale apiece to wash it down, then set off, with the good lucks of the others ringing in our ears. From the outside, I suppose we looked like any band of animals off on a jaunt, allowing only that our motor car was a weird one. But the feeling inside was most peculiar. We was all excited, and jumpy, and a touch fearful. We was off on a jaunt to a prison. There to take and spirit away a criminal of deepest die. Perhaps to be pursued, and hunted, and shot at. Perhaps to save the whole notion of Brotherhood Hall. It was a desperate mission. Despite the sunshine, despite the sheer pleasure of bowling along in a motor car, we were a grim and silent group.

We'd only got well under halfway, still with very little having been said by way of conversation, when something in Turner's manner, along of something my own ears had been a-telling me, made me and that stoat look at each other. What I saw in his eyes made my heart sink. It wasn't my imagination, for sure.

'Listen, Turner,' says I. 'I'm right, ain't I? There's something like a rattle and a clatter starting up down there. There's something that sounds like—'

No point in going on with that one. With a startling suddenness, the almost inaudible rattling turned into a full-scale, metallic, frightening din. I hit the brakes with all my might and the stoat, who'd been leaning forward to get a better listen, banged his snout on the screen hard and rapid.

Then we all got out and stood in the road, looking at the engine, which I'd turned off.

There was nothing to see, no steam or smoke or nothing. But Turner and me, we had a fair idea of what was up. It sounded to us like the big-ends gone.

'Is it serious?' asked Harrison. He pulled a big turnip of a watch from his pocket and glared at it like the passage of time was its fault and its alone. 'We've not got much time to muck about with, Baxter.'

'My dear chap,' said Radcliffe. 'With two mechanical geniuses like our friends here on hand, we've not a care in the world. You mark my words, we'll be bowling along again in half a jiffy.'

Turner swung the handle and started her, without a word. We listened to the heavy clunk clunk. It was unbearable.

'Switch off, Turner,' I said. 'Switch off do. I can't abide it.'

For I knew, and Turner knew, and Harrison, even Radcliffe Weasel guessed, that Baxter's Flying Column had bit the dust. There we was, between here and nowhere, without a chance in twenty of moving again that day.

'What we going to do, Captain?' Harrison asked, when I told them what I thought. 'Can we make it on foot? And if we do, can we get him and hold him, does you think?'

I sat beside the road with my head in my hands. If only we'd had more time to check the mechanicals. If only Dolly hadn't switched her plan and gone a day early to the jail. If only the worst possible fault hadn't happened. My mind was in a whirl.

Turner Stoat tapped me on the shoulder. He'd been rooting around in the capacious toolbox.

'We've got spare shells, sir,' he said. 'We've got two jacks, and all the tools. We might be able to do it, given luck. We might get her back on the road.'

'Spare shells! Turner Stoat, you're a good man! When did you put them in?'

He smiled.

'Well sir, I knew you was busy and being messed about like, so I got up an emergency kit. I put in a spare set of everything I could think of. Spare shells was about the first things I hit on, natural-like.'

Harrison and Radcliffe were mystified. Spare shells meant nothing to them. They just wanted to know if we could get the A.S.P. on the move again.

'Listen, you animals,' I told them. 'We've got the makings to put this job right, temporary at least. The big-end bearings has gone, which is serious and no mistake. But we've got new shell bearings and the tools to fit 'em. Time ain't on our side, to say the least of it. But we might do it. Turner here—' Turner had actually disappeared. He was already under the car, jacking up the front wheels and engine so as we could crawl under easier. 'Turner here and me might just – oh forget it. Look, one of you's got to get back to Toad Hall and warn O.B. If we can't get to the jail in time, I don't know what'll happen. But he's got to know, in case he can come up with a plan. Now; who's to go?'

We hit on Radcliffe in the end, because although he was slower and fatter than Harrison, he was pretty fit and agile from all his dancing and prancing. Also the ferret, being a gunsmith and good with his hands, could probably be a help to me and my mate. Within minutes the slightly tubby, slightly dandyish weasel was disappearing round a bend in the leafy road at a jogtrot. If he didn't happen on a lift, he'd a long way to jog. But he was sure he could do it.

It was a long, hard, hot job on the crippled motor car, and we had precious little time to do it in. We stripped down to our shirtsleeves, then to our vests. Our smart clothes, worn to hide the serious, not to say illegal, nature of our business at the prison, was soon dirty, torn and streaked with grease. Harrison proved an apt pupil, and we worked as a team. Silent, sweating, determined.

But what a task, when all's said! We'd to jack up the front, take off the sump without losing no oil, get the retaining pins and *oodles* of nuts and bolts off, marking each one's position so that it went back exactly the same, get out the old babbit-metal shells, fit new ones, snug 'em into the journals and wiggle and prod till they fitted right, make sure that all was – well, you get the picture. By the time we had the engine back in one piece again, we was oil, dirt and sweat from tail-ends to nose-tips, and what's more it was getting dark. Only just, and hardly so that it showed. But evening was definitely drawing in. We could imagine that even now Dolly would be 'playing the washerwoman' with Toad. That even now he would be tying her up and telling himself what a clever chap he was, and how he was going to walk out a free animal. I looked at the sinking sun in despair. It looked dreadfully as though he might do just that very thing.

The engine started with a roar, and we set off at a breakneck speed. Fitting new shell bearings to big-ends isn't often one hundred per cent. Unless you treats them with kid gloves, like, they often goes again. But I could only drive and hope. That strange, homemade vehicle got flogged like a racer. I screamed round corners on two wheels, shot across dicey junctions with my hand on the klaxon and my heart in my mouth, went over humpback bridges at such a rate that we took right off, and flew for yards at a time. The new shells took it like a dream, but me and Turner and Harrison wasn't so happy at all. It was a terrifying drive.

By the time we got to the jail, it was full dark. I eased up the engine and we coasted the last few yards quiet like, till finally we stopped near the main gate in deep shadow, on the opposite side of the road. In the pause after that mad drive, our breathing sounded loud and unnatural. All three of us was panting with anticipation, and not a little fear left over from what we'd been through. None of us spoke, but the same thought filled all our heads. Was we in time?

After about ten minutes the little wicket gate in the vast, black gates of the castle swung open. We went tense, our eyes popping out of our skulls. It was a female. She looked about her uncertainly, then set off towards the town. I breathed a great sigh of relief, and slipped into bottom gear. The A.S.P. rolled forward almost silent, and as we caught up with the hurrying figure, Turner and Harrison opened their doors, ready to spring out. At the right moment I braked hard and shouted: 'All right lads! Grab him!'

The stoat and the ferret seized the woman, clapped a hand over her mouth, and hauled her bodily into the car, kicking like fury and trying to scream. Slam went the doors, down went my boot on the pedal, away shot the car at a tremendous lick. I looked in the mirror, but there was no sign of pursuit. I was jubilant.

'Well boys,' I cried. 'We've done it! Let his mouth free and let's see what the vile creature's got to say for himself. Hello, Toadie! How are you feeling now, eh?'

The voice that answered sent such a shock through me that I nearly drove up a tree.

'Baxter,' it said evenly. 'You are a fool. Oh Baxter, you *are* a fool. Toad left an hour ago. Don't tell me you weren't there to meet him. *Please* don't tell me that.'

It was our Dolly. Oh dear, I tell you true. It was my little sister. And Toad had escaped.

Chapter Nineteen

THE CHASE

'The daft thing is,' said O.B., 'that if it hadn't been for us, Toad would still be in there. Now he's out, and we're in dead trouble. Dead trouble.'

'It was a daft scheme. A mad scheme. I knew no good would come of it.' That was the stoat speaking, as you'd guess. He was ignored.

'But what are we going to do, that's the question. Oh O.B., what *are* we going to do?' That was Dolly, wringing her hands in a very worried fashion indeed.

It was late the same night, and we were having an emergency staff meeting in the big study. When we'd finally got back to the Hall, covered in grease and confusion, so to speak, O.B. had got over the first shock long since. He didn't blame me in any way, being more interested in saving the situation than chewing over what had went wrong. As soon as Radcliffe Weasel had puffed up the carriage drive with the news, he'd done a lot of hard thinking, and come up with what he called Plan B.

The reasoning behind it was this. Toad had got clean away, fair enough. Now, if he managed to evade capture by the law, he'd go to one of three places. Firstly Toad Hall. But O.B. ruled that out, even for such a dim and foolish article as Toadie. If he knew that we'd taken it over he'd obviously not turn up on his own, and if he didn't know he'd still avoid it like the plague for fear the police might go there looking for the jailbreaker. Secondly, Badger's place, where he could be sure of food, drink, a welcome, and protection. But Badger's was in the Wild Wood, which area the cowardly animal would probably rather die than enter on his own. If he did, by some chance, he'd likely find it empty in any case, for the Badger spent most of his nights along of the Mole, keeping an eye on the big house. Thirdly, and most likely, Toad'd go to Rat's place on the River Bank. Now, if he found the quarters empty and abandoned, so to speak, what on earth would he do? He'd be fair jiggered.

At first, therefore, O.B. had toyed with the idea of kidnapping Rat by force to clear him out of his hole – but he'd quickly scrapped it. For a start-off, with the future of our whole venture very uncertain, it wasn't a good plan to indulge in any more acts that might be judged criminal. Especially if Toadie ever got the law back on his side!

Finally, and after a deal of thought, O.B. had called in Wilson. And potty as the suggestion he made him sounds, it danged nearly worked. The sea rat had dressed up in a weird collection of his old clothes, stuck a pair of rings in his ears like he was still a mariner, tied up a couple of things in a kerchief as though he was a wanderer on the tramp, and set off to see if he couldn't find Ratty. He did, almost at once – and in a dreamy, poety sort of mood to boot.

Now Wilson, as you know, had a great way with tales, and stories, and such. He cracked on to Rat that he was a seafaring fellow, as had tried to swallow the anchor, but had quickly had a bellyful of shore life and was heading for the ocean again. He yarned on about the South, and the sun, and the romance and the freedom, till he had that poor silly country rat seeing himself as Captain Cook or someone. All nonsense, but none the worse for that – for the joke is that Wilson was much happier talking about the sea than he'd ever been working on it!

He must have been good, though, for when he wandered off romantic-like, towards the South, he was certain sure that Rat was going to follow him. In fact he would have, Wilson said, for the old shop-keeper skirted back once he'd got out of sight, and watched Rat's hole. After a time the door opened and out he came, dressed for the road, with a knapsack and a daft look on his mug. And just at that very same moment, along come the Mole and spoiled it all. He saw immediate that something was up, grabbed Rat like a sack of spuds, and shoved him back inside. Fighting like mad to join old Wilson on the road to the sea! What a laugh!

'The trouble is,' said O.B. 'Funny as it may have been, it means we failed. Rat's still at home, and Mole's probably with him, keeping an eye, like. So if Toad goes there, he's done us.'

It was late on now, and disaster or no disaster, I had to run Dolly home in the A.S.P. As we headed towards the study door, there was a knock on it. It was Radcliffe, excited as you like.

'Intelligence have picked up a report, sir,' he said, to the Chief Weasel. 'Toad's been spotted. He's in a wood some miles off, near the railway. He was seen by a fox called Johnson, and an owl, name unknown. Oh yes, he's still in his togs. Johnson apparently thought he was a washerwoman, but he may have been joking. You know what foxes are.'

O.B.'s eyes gleamed.

'Do we know where he is now?'

'No, sir. That was about two hours ago. The owl's been patrolling the area since, but no sign of him.'

When Radcliffe had gone, we talked it out. We had another chance, and we had to take it, fast. But for all that, O.B. decided not to make any more moves till morning. We was all tired, we'd probably not find him, and we'd need to be right on the button from daybreak onwards. Better to leave it till then.

The morning dawned bright and warm. I was up with the lark, but Turner had beat me to it. The engine of the A.S.P. was warmed up and ticking over ready to go. By the time I arrived back with Dolly, the first intelligence had come in. Toad had been spotted almost as soon as he'd left his bolt-hole. He'd hitched a lift on a canal barge. Some miles away, but heading in the right direction – towards the river.

'Well, O.B.,' I asked. 'What's the plan? We can't very well kidnap him off of a barge, can we?'

He shook his head.

'Too true, Bax my boy. We'll have to wait and see. But we'll have to wait close-to, so as we can nab him the minute he gets off.'

'Well, that canal meets up with the river, according to the maps,' said Boddington Stoat. 'I wonder if he'll come all the way, or hop off early, like.'

'Probably all the way,' said the Chief. 'But the barge won't come on to the river, I shouldn't think. He'll probably be dropped off near the junction.'

'What about being captured?' Dolly said. 'Won't he be expecting the police to be keeping an eye out? He'll most likely get off a distance inland, and walk the rest. He'd be trapped too easy on a barge.'

This was good thinking. Clearly, we had to keep an eye on the last stretch of canal, plus the stretch close to the river itself.

'Well, Bax,' O.B. laughed. 'How's the old banger, then? Think it'll blow up on you again?'

'Seems to be running all right,' I replied. 'Sweet as a bell, that old engine sounds today.'

'Righto, then. The Flying Column can go to the bridge about two mile inland. He won't get off afore then. After his boat's gone past, follow along quiet like. The road's beside the canal there, ain't it?'

We checked the map. It was, as we all knew. Better safe than sorry this time, though.

'Now, as soon as Toad gets off that barge, nab him. No messing about, just nab him and whip him back here smartish, got it? Take the same crew as you took yesterday, only this time don't let anything go wrong. Boddington here'll take a contingent to where the river and the canal meets in case he goes all the way. If that happens, drop as many of your men as is needed to make room, and bring Boddington and Toad back immediate. I'll stay here, worse luck, in case there's any new developments. I miss all the fun. We've got a team of runners ready and waiting today, to keep you informed of any changes of plan.'

It was very pleasant sitting on the canal bridge in the sunshine, pretending to fish. Turner had the car hidden in a thicket, ready to go at the signal. Me and Radcliffe and Harrison dangled our legs over the parapet, with lengths of string on sticks trailing in the water. There was very little traffic, just two or three boats passed us. But we knew the colours and marks of the one we was waiting for.

'I tell you what,' said Radcliffe, after a good old time had gone past. 'That barge isn't hurrying, and that's a fact.'

Before I had time to answer there was a rustling and crashing of undergrowth nearby. Out burst a young stoat, panting fit to bust. When he'd got his breath back he gasped out his message, that had us racing for the car like billy-oh. Toad had done it again. He'd given us the slip.

The full story, as told by O.B., was amazing. Not only had Toad got off the barge, but he'd been thrown off. Our animals had talked to the bargee's wife. There'd been a row, it seemed, and she'd chucked Toad overboard. That desperate animal, to get his own back, had stolen her horse and made off. The boat, out of control, had gone aground and was still stuck fast.

'But where is he now?' I said. 'How will we catch him if we don't know where he is?'

'Patience, Bax boy,' said O.B. 'We do know where he is, or near enough. After he'd gone off on the horse, it seems he wandered about a good piece, not knowing exactly where he was, like, and being too much of a fool to follow the canal. Finally he come up to a Gypsy, as who our scouts have spoken to. Toad sold him the woman's horse for six and a tanner, plus all the breakfast he could eat (which was apparently about a week's supply, at that), then set off on a route as the traveller pointed out to him. Now, me and Dolly have worked out that route, from this end to the point where he left the Gypsy. So get her started up, lad, and we'll catch him yet.'

Dolly got into the front in place of Turner, who squeezed in the back with Radcliffe and Harrison. When we caught Toad, one or two of 'em would have to walk back. I didn't relish the idea of my sister coming on such a desperate mission, but O.B. had to stay at the Hall to overlord things, whereas Dolly was able to manage the directions better than anyone else. She soon had the big coloured map spread over her knees, and we was away.

We flew down highways and byways, following the complicated course that the Gypsy had set for Toad. If only he kept to it, we'd be all right. But would he, that was the question? If he didn't, that foolish animal would get hopelessly lost. If he did, he'd fall directly into our hands.

It was late morning when we at last came upon Toad, and at first we didn't know it. As we rounded a bend in the road the glaring sun caught me full in the eyes. I slowed down, pulling the peak of my cap lower. When I could see again, I realised there had been an accident. An old woman lay in the road a couple of hundred yards ahead. Around her stood a group of people, three or four of them. Behind them all was a motor car.

As we slowly drew nearer – I was planning to stop, of course, to see if we could help – the woman was lifted into the car, gentle as could be. We were alongside as her old head lolled back, causing her bonnet to fall away from her face. Dolly let out a muffled shriek, stuffing her paw into her mouth to cut it off.

'It's him!' she said. 'It's Toad! Quick Bax, turn round! We've found him!'

By the time I had manoeuvred the A.S.P. about-face in that narrow country lane, the car that had picked up the bogus washerwoman had rounded the bend at quite a lick. I pressed the accelerator to the floor and gave our vehicle her head. Round the curve the quarry was just a speck.

'Go on, Bax,' urged Dolly. 'We've got to catch up. We've *got* to, for the sake of Brotherhood Hall.'

Soon the hedges became a blur as we whizzed along. Every time we rounded a bend, the motor car in front was nearer. This time he couldn't escape! I gritted my teeth in concentration, getting every last ounce of speed possible. We was positively flying. With the quarry only a hundred yards in front, we could see Toad plain. He was sitting up in the big open car now, lively as a cricket. I throttled back. We had him. Let that motor car just stop and let him out, and Toad was ours.

The big-ends went then. Just like that. Those poor overworked shells, that we'd fitted the day before and flogged so unmerciful, just gave up the ghost. Funny that they should wait until I slowed down, after lasting throughout the chase. Funny!? It was tragic.

We clattered and clanked our way to a halt, and I switched off the ruins of the engine. We watched the car, and Toad, dwindle and disappear into the shimmering heat-hazed distance, without a word being said. Then Dolly burst into tears.

By the time we'd trudged the weary miles back to headquarters, the full story was known, except for our part in it. Somehow or other that hadn't been made clear, Toad had got into the driving seat of the car, whether by force or subterfuge is impossible to tell. He apparently became crazed at his own skill and the vehicle's great power, and finally crashed it through a hedge and into a pond. He'd been chased, both by the motoring party and a couple of passing policemen, but had reached the river before them.

Toads, even fat and indolent toads like Toad, can swim better than most policemen. So he had escaped. Worse still, the place he'd gone into the river was not a big distance from Rat's house. So it was a pound to a penny that our enemy, thanks to nobody but ourselves, had reached comfort and safety once more.

O.B. looked at us gloomily when he'd finished the tale. Then he said one sentence.

'It's enough to make you sick.'

Chapter Twenty
'TIS DARK AND LURKS THE NAUGHTY DEED'

When we got Toad out of prison, the Chief Weasel had said, we'd have a feast. Well, we'd got him out, and no mistake.

But imagine everyone's amazement when it was announced that the banquet would go ahead as planned, the very next night. Boddington Stoat was so furious he called a meeting of the general staff on the spot.

'It's an outrage,' he shrieked. 'It's an absolute outrage. It's like Nero fiddling while Rome burnt down around his earholes. Toad's back with his friends. There'll be an attack at any minute. At the very least he might try to have the law on us. You'm puddled, Weasel! You'm absolutely puddled!'

That Toad was back with his friends, was no longer a matter of guesswork. The very afternoon that he'd crashed the motor car and evaded the police, he'd marched up to the main gates of Brotherhood Hall as bold as brass, carrying a great stick to beat us out of it single-handed. By this time the discipline, drill, keenness etcetera of the troops was button bright again, on account of the goings on as had been going on. A ferret sentry had challenged Toad, then fired a pot shot over his head and sent him scurrying. The foolish creature had tried again, however, this time by water. But as he'd rowed his boat under the boat-house creek bridge, a couple of stoats had dropped a dirty big stone through the bottom of it, after which he apparently learnt that we meant business, or was restrained by his friends, or something. They was now lurking back at Rat's, as we guessed, plotting and planning their next move.

O.B. smiled at the blazing angry stoat, not losing his temper a scrap. In fact he might have been enjoying himself, I reckon. He hooked his thumbs into his plum velvet waistcoat, waiting for Boddington to fizzle out. As soon as he had, the Chief said something calculated to set him off once more.

'Now now, Boddie, don't blow your safety valve, lad. The banquet must go on, you know. We can't let one little setback spoil the fun, now can we?'

The dour animal turned from puce to white to puce to grey. He shook. My sister went and tried to hold his hand, but he flapped her off him like a moth. When he could speak, it was in a whisper that was more a hiss. I felt most uncomfortable, and wished miserably that I might be allowed to go and tinker with an engine or something.

'It's a betrayal, Weasel,' he said. 'A betrayal. And I'll tell you one thing. I won't have nothing to do with it, nor will none of my stoats. We took Brotherhood Hall for the good of all, not to provide feasts and parties for a bloke what turns out to be worse than the criminal Toad hisself.'

O.B.'s grin broadened, although my jaw muscles was aching with tension.

'But Bodd,' he said, in a taunting kind of way. 'It's my birthday today. You wouldn't want me to miss my party, would you? I always has a party, don't I, Baxter?'

I jumped as though prodded with a sharp stick, but luckily never had time to answer. Boddington was off again, and this time he proper got into his stride.

'Right from the very start it's been the same,' he ranted. 'You said you'd come into it on account of Toad and Co needed taking down, on account of their vicious and criminal misuse of other animals' wealth. But you never meant it. As soon as we got here you was just like him, only worse. You had no idea of making things better for the poor Wild Wooders. You just liked it for the fun of the fight, and the smell of the kitchens and larders. You didn't fight for us or our poor friends, you fought on account of you liked it. You're a warlord, that's what. An easy-going, wine-bibbing, good-eating, late-drinking, self-important, self-satisfied, conceited warlord. You're like Toad! You're just like Toad! You're *worse* than Toad! And I bet you won't even care if he comes back and takes over again. You'll probably join him.'

There was a long silence after the stoat had run down. Silence, that is, except for his heavy breathing. Even that had quietened before O.B. spoke.

'Well, Captain Boddington,' he said. 'I'm sorry you feel unable to join in our little bit of fun tonight. At least the security of being guarded by you and your excellent stoats will make the party go with an even greater swing. As to the rest of it. Well, perhaps we'd better have a serious talk tomorrow. It appears to me, like, that you've gone a little touch too far. You're almost, as I see it, calling me a traitor. Now that, Captain Boddington, is rather strong words in my book. Especially about your Chief.'

I'm ready to swear that the stoat would have gone off on another how-do-you-do, but he was prevented by a knock at the door. It was Radcliffe, leading a very jittery stoat sergeant.

'This chap's got something to tell you, sir,' he told O.B. 'Something about an attack tonight or somesuch.'

'Tell me! Tell me!' said Boddington eagerly.

'Shut up and listen,' said the Chief Weasel. 'Now, sergeant. What is it?'

The sergeant was practically incoherent, with a mixture of excitement and the jitters. But we worked out, in the end, that a washerwoman who 'did' for Badger, or whose relations did or something, had come to the guardhouse offering to take in the sentries' washing. The sergeant, so he said, had been immediately suspicious, and questioned her. Finally she'd revealed that Toad's friends had got together a veritable army. Hundreds of badgers, boatload after boatload of rats, a battalion of toads. They were to attack Brotherhood Hall tonight.

'Where is she, then?' asked the Chief Weasel. 'Where is this so-called washerwoman?'

'Beg to report sir, she escaped sir. Run away sir. Very fleet of foot she was sir, all things considered.'

O.B. dismissed him without a word, despite his serious and obvious failure to detain an important source of intelligence. When the door closed, Boddington weighed straight in.

'Now will you see sense?' he said. 'How can you even dream of banqueting, in face of that?'

'It do seem serious, like,' I added. 'Don't you think perhaps, O.B.? I mean, all them badgers and so on.'

'Yes, funny, isn't it,' mused my friend. 'Yesterday or the day before it was a chimney sweep, wasn't it? Now it's a washerwoman. There's a lot of 'em about, it seems to me.'

'Sweep?' says I. 'What sweep? A lot of what about?'

Dolly give me a strained smile.

'While we was out springing Toad,' she said. 'An otter came to the hall claiming to be a sweep. O.B. thinks he was a spy.'

'Thinks!' said Boddington angrily. 'Don't *know* mark you, just thinks. And now I suppose he "thinks" this woman's one, too, and we don't have to heed her words.'

'Well, anyway,' said O.B. 'If she was an old lady she must have been a spry one, you will allow. Being questioned by a dozen nippy stoats, yet she manages to run away. I hope I'm that fit when I'm in my dotage, that's all.'

'We can't risk it,' said Boddington. 'We can't risk it. What if there was an attack tonight? We must double the guard. Treble 'em. You must call off the banquet.'

The Chief Weasel didn't move a muscle. After a while Dolly said, in a tired, dull sort of voice, 'I think I'll go home now. I'll see you all in the morning.'

Boddington turned on her, eyes pink.

'So you don't believe me, neither! You think the feast should go on, and we'll all be here tomorrow, right as ninepence?'

'Oh Bod,' Dolly replied wearily. 'I just don't know. At the moment I can't think. All I want to do is go home and rest.'

While the grey-coated stoat walked her to the main gates, O.B. and me sat down in the study. I blew out a long whistley breath through my lips. What a meeting that had been, and no mistake! We both said nowt for a while, relaxing like.

'Anyway,' I started, at long last. 'What do you truly think, O.B.? Could there be an attack? If there really is that number of ferocious badgers on the warpath, do you reckon we could hold 'em off?'

'Baxter, boy, there ain't that many badgers in the whole county, you mark my words. And if there was, and they was on the march, don't you think we'd have got a whiff of 'em? Not one report's come in of any troop movements.'

'Why do you taunt that Boddington, then?' I asked. 'He's as jumpy as a bug.'

'That's why, then,' laughed O.B. 'Them stoats takes it all so dead serious, like. It gets on my nerves. Spoils the fun. So I likes to give 'em the jitters. And if there *should* be an attack tonight,' he added, serious like. 'If there *should* be, I say. Well – they'll be ready for it, and no messing, eh?'

I thought for a while, watching my handsome, brightly dressed friend with interest. The devilment in his character was coming out strong these days, I could tell. He'd missed most of the action on the Toad plan, and that had made him very restless.

'What do you think'll happen now?' I asked. 'I mean, about the Hall and everything. They're not going to hang about long like, are they? They'll attack soon, for sure. Can we hold out?'

O.B. leaned towards me and lowered his voice, although Lord knows the study was soundproof enough.

'Listen, Baxter,' he said. 'You're my mate, eh? My best friend. I'll tell you something that I'd not tell no one else. Mustn't go no further, naturally.'

I nodded, very pleased at the confidence.

'Well,' he went on. 'The way I see it, there's bound to be trouble, and it's bound to be soon. It may be tonight even, I don't know. And whether we can hold out, or how long, I don't know either. But I tell you what, Bax. I'd rather have trouble than go on like this. Between you and me and the gate-post, I'm fed up to the back teeth with it. It's all very well that daft stoat talking about brotherhood, and equality, and suchlike, but I'm bored silly. It'll be Christmas before too much longer, and I know where I'd rather be, don't you? Hang Christmas – it'll be Brewday even sooner! Are we to be stuck in this draughty old pile of masonry when we could be at your hole knocking back your ma's barley wine? Eh?'

It was a thought, and no mistake! A sudden wave of longing flooded over me. I hadn't had a clout from Daisy for as long as I could recall. Billy Bingo; and how I missed it!

O.B. got more animated.

'The way I see it, Baxter, this banquet tonight'll be our last fling, one way and another. For there's something else as is not known except by me and the head cook and Cecil the cellarman. The grub we'll be eating tonight, and the drink we'll be drinking, is just about the lot. No, honest – keeping a garrison the size of ours goes through food and drink in next to no time flat. If that Toad and his friends don't make a move soon, we might even have to make one ourselves. Like pulling out, for example!'

This was staggering. My mouth dropped open.

'No, that's daft,' O.B. laughed. 'Never say die, eh? I'm just being silly. But we will have to make some sort of move, Baxter. We'll have to go out foraging for grub. Maybe do a bit more—' He paused, shaking his head. 'But I don't reckon so, you know. I reckon we'll see some action soon. Sooner than you think, perhaps.'

'What do you mean?' I asked. 'How soon? Do you know something O.B.? Have you heard something?'

But he just shook his head again, and smiled. Looking, maybe, as though he'd said more than he meant to.

The rest of the day was spent in preparing for the banquet, and a jolly fine one it was going to be, and all. If O.B. had been telling me straight about the state of the larder and cellar, he certainly meant to make the clear-out complete.

The quantity of meat and poultry cooked, the dozen upon dozen hot loaves that came in batches out of the ovens, the case after case of wine brought up from below to be ready for drinking; it was fair amazing.

Everyone was in a very festive mood, singing and laughing as the preparations went ahead. Only the stoats took no part in it. They were in a black bad humour, mooching around in full battle order, doubling up here, trebling up at the weakest parts of the perimeter wall, cleaning rifles, testing their side-arms. When a weasel or a ferret ran into one of 'em, there was usually an exchange – bantering on the one side, bitter on the other. The Chief Weasel wasn't much in evidence. I think he was up in his room, getting his gayest clothes out and brushed, making sure his batman got the shine on his boots just so, composing speeches and songs, and practising new tunes on his concertina.

From the very first moment, the banquet was a humdinger. The food was delicious, and course followed course so fast that I soon felt like I was going to explode. We drank wine like it was water, and most of us even filled in the gaps between courses with tankards of excellent ale, drawn fresh from the cellar by Cecil. It was a pretty disgusting display of gluttony, one way and another, when I comes to look back on it. But at the time, it seemed the only thing; living like lords, drinking like donkeys, eating like pigs.

When we'd stuffed ourselves to a standstill, so to speak, we sat back in our chairs, panting and incapable, to listen to the speech that O.B., we knew, was bound to make. He was a witty speaker, and we was in the mood for it. Not a hand as didn't have a glass in, not a belt as hadn't been loosened a notch or three. Practically every word he said (and I'm blowed if I can remember one of them) was greeted with a roar, or a cheer, or a gale of laughter. We stamped and hooted, banged and chinked our glasses, it was a riot. Finally he came to an end, except for the song. Like most of the speech, it was to be on the subject of Toad, that infamous animal who had provided us so generously with food, drink and laughter.

It was almost like a signal. O.B. took a deep draught of wine, wiped his whiskers with the back of his hand, filled his lungs, and burst forth. Before he'd finished the first line, practically, the door shot open with an almighty crash that near took it off its hinges, and the room seemed to be filled with roaring, bellowing, furious animals. The attack had come.

I happened to be watching the Chief Weasel's face when it all started, and it was most odd. He was drunk, granted, drunk as it's possible to be. But he can't have realised what was going on at all, for he smiled, I swear it. A slow, happy smile spread across his chops – and stayed there. Until a clout from a stick knocked him off of his chair clean over the table. In the seconds before my own head was knocked almost off my shoulders and I begun to see nowt but stars, I had time to register who'd whacked O.B. It was Toad. Ah well, I thought, as I sank to my knees, even a worm can turn.

The rest of the evening's completely confused in my head like, on account of the blow I'd been give. There was screaming, and yelling, and rushing about. It's a racing cert that no one was in a fit condition to put up a fight, for obvious reasons, and how I got out I haven't the foggiest idea. But a short time later, I found myself in the gardens, being half dragged, half carried by Radcliffe Weasel and Harrison Ferret. At some stage I recall being punched on the nose by a stoat, who appeared to think we were attacking him, but it's pretty blurry, to tell the truth. Somehow or other I got home and got to bed, as did nearly everyone else, I learned later. Even the prisoners taken by Toad's party was released the same night. Too drunk to be worth keeping, I suppose.

So there it was. Captain Baxter was a mere ferret again. And Brotherhood Hall, after a few glorious weeks, belonged once more to its master. Toad.

Chapter Twenty-one
GOODBYE DOLLY

The next morning when I went downstairs to the kitchen, having risen very late on account of my splitting headache, my ma was sitting by herself, staring into the kitchen fire. Although she'd had to accept certain things, what with Dolly living there and me visiting occasional, she'd always hated the whole affair, and she'd aged considerable over that summer, had Daisy. Today she looked positively exhausted. The kids was not in evidence, by sight or sound, although I'm sure I don't know where they was. I sat down quiet like, pouring myself out a cup of tea. It was funny, I'd expected her to be glad, one way and another.

'What's up then, our ma?' I asked after a while. 'It's all over now, you know. Right or wrong we've been beat, and you've got us back again. It'll be a long time before I get caught up in such doings again, I can promise you.'

Ma stared on, poking feebly at the fire in the way she did when down. She sniffed a little, too, like she was almost crying.

'I'll try and find a job,' I said. 'There'll be harvesting and so on, so I bet I'll soon be earning a bob or two. Dolly'll likely find a position as well, now she's that bit older.'

Ma looked at me for the first time. Her eyes was dull, and slowly filled with tears as I watched.

'Dolly?' she said. 'Dolly won't... Dolly...' She choked on a sob, and run from the room. I followed after a while, but didn't dare go in her bedroom, for she was weeping something pitiful, and I knew she'd want to be alone.

It all came out soon enough, of course. Early that morning, Boddington Stoat had come for Dolly. He was heading North, he said, before Toad had us all jailed for life. In any case, the Chief Weasel, he reckoned, was a traitor that had betrayed the Wild Wooders, and been the direct cause of our downfall. He was going to Manchester to help the animals there in the depressed industrial zones to fight for their liberty and suchlike.

He asked once more for Dolly's hand, polite and respectable, but my mother wouldn't hear of it and blew her top. My sister, apparently, had been torn something cruel. But when Ma had got hysterical, and said some hard and nasty things about not wanting any grandchilder of hern to be 'foats' or 'sterrets' or somesuch, Dolly had seen red. Their love, right or wrong, she'd cried. And gone off with Boddington.

Of course, the talk of betrayal was all my-eye. The guard-stoats had thought they'd been attacked from the inside by the rest of us, while we thought they must've let Toad's party in, secret like. But it turned out later that there was an underground passage that Toad's father had once told the Badger about, being too wise to let his own son know! The armed band had got right into the heart of the house with no one a jot the wiser. It was too easy.

As for us all being flung into jail, well it just didn't happen, nor to Toad, neither. The way of it was, according to O.B., was this: When Toad got free, he immediately brought his wealth and influence to bear on the police and the local justices; a piece of cake apparently, especially because us Wooders was hardly in a position to make a fuss about it. By the same token, though, Toad could hardly try to get us brought to court, or the gallows, because of the stink it would have caused; the quieter everyone kept about his escape and continued freedom the better. People might have started to think the law was corrupt, or something dreadful like that.

What's more, because of O.B.'s brilliant way of getting to the heart of such situations, he'd actually got to talk with Toad, and brought off a deal. In return for nothing being said all round, a lot of the injustices of life between the River Bankers and the Wild Wooders was ironed out. Some of Toad's surplus wealth went to providing more and better jobs like, and he introduced pensions and so on, and stopped sacking people for pique, or in slack times. The trump card was that the silly animal never knew that he'd been sprung from jail by us – he thought it was his own cleverness! If he'd ever been able to tell the police of our part in it, and thus deny his own criminal intent, I suppose he could have had us jailed in a jiffy. But as you know, we're a crafty, secret folk, so he never even guessed.

One way and another, then, life pretty soon got back to normal, or better. I was took on as the Toad Hall chauffeur and mechanic, with Turner Stoat as my assistant. What's more, I got to drive till my heart's content. For I'll say this of my employer. Silly he might have remained (did, in fact), but he never took the wheel of a motor in his life again. He was a reformed character.

My friend O.B., the Chief Weasel, who'd been his arch enemy and the improver of our lot, gradually got closer and closer in with the squire, aye, and his chums as well. In fact it wasn't that long before I often found myself driving O.B. home to the Wild Wood after he'd been an honoured guest at a ball, or a banquet, or a feast or somesuch. Tell the truth, it wasn't all that much longer that O.B. bought himself a summer house by the river. Only a summer house, mind; he was still our beloved and loyal chief. O.B. was not the animal to desert his friends, though we did miss his concertina-playing something dreadful at first, on Brewdays, and at Christmas and so on.

All in all, life settled down very nice and comfortable, thanks very much. The only real trouble was Dolly, who we never looked to see again, and my ma, who never got over that sad loss. She used to cry a lot, and aged very rapid, despite the increased comfort of our lives and no more money worries. Years later I heard that my sister had indeed married Boddington, and started a small brewery to finance his political activities. Whether he'd managed to alleviate the hardships of the poor or not, I'm in no position to say, but Dolly, by turning out fine bitter beer to my mother's recipe, must certainly have done, and the ale's still brewed there, folks who live up North have told me. But I missed her very hard I did, for I loved my sister dearly.

Looking back on those days, I'm still a bit mystified by it all. Things got better after the Toad Hall episode, true, but I'm jiggered if I understands the ins and outs of it. Some of the Wild Wooders got even more humble and kowtowish after Toad and Co recaptured the big house, while others, like the Chief Weasel say, become almost as posh as they was.

One thing I am sure of, though. Speaking purely personal, like (and I reckon I ought to be a bit ashamed of it, maybe), I never got settled to the life like what I'd used to be. There was peace all right, but there was something else too. Regret's the nearest to it I can think of, but I'm probably wrong. I never did understand it all, really. Not so's you'd notice…

Epilogue
'THE MAD OLD GENTLEMAN'
(OR HOW THE STORY CAME TO LIGHT)

'And so a gallant band was formed, to bring about the downfall of the rich uncaring few. They were the Wild Wood Volunteers, and theirs is a saga of poverty and desperation, loyalty and treachery, strange love and great despair.'

Thus did my poor friend Cedric Willoughby, journalist, bonviveur and *soi disant* great historian, introduce Baxter Ferret's story to me, as he lay on his bed of pain. Cedric Willoughby, I

215

hear you ask? Who the devil might he be when he's home? Well, the truth is, he will be at home no more, ever. Piecing together the story of what he called 'this rural holocaust' exhausted him completely, and blighted the last months of his life.

Most tragically of all, it was a minor thing that did for him – he lacked a sense of direction. As the 'mad old gent' who 'ran into' the ferret at the crossroads near his cosy hole, he assumed that he could find his way back there again if the need arose. It did, and Cedric didn't. After frantic searching, he fell into a deep depression, that led him to a deeper one yet – in his local graveyard.

Although they had met in difficult circumstances, these two odd individuals actually became quite close for a poignantly short time. They shared the ferret's homely quarters while he fixed the motor car, and yarned and gossiped over home-brewed ale and suppers in the evenings. Then, while Baxter slept, Cedric toiled away on page after page of notes, that he passionately believed would become his *magnum opus*.

So grandiose were his plans, in fact, that he rapidly decided he needed much more than a pen and laptop to do his subject justice. He envisaged trendy historians, camera crews, and correspondents from the Times, the Telegraph, and possibly the Guardian (if they promised to behave). In the centre of this media frenzy would be Cedric Willoughby and his dear chum Baxter, the smartest ferret in the Wood. They would be serenely famous.

Sadly, though, Cedric had never learned to calibrate the satnav that was fitted to his vintage motor car. The lady's voice was pleasant, her directions incomprehensible. She piloted him to every wood, and copse, and thicket in the South of England, and all to no avail. He never saw that hole, or possibly indeed that county, ever again.

I promised Cedric, before he breathed his last, that I would make a detailed study of his writings, with a view to drawing socio/psychological conclusions for the brightest brains of *academe* to ponder over – but I won't. I fear my friend's obsession had got a little out of control by the time of his demise, and some things are better left unsaid. Willoughby was born, and died, eccentric. He also drank like a rather thirsty fish.

Even the way he met his friendly ferret was distinctly *louche*. It happened on the annual London to Brighton Veteran Car Run – and not to put too fine a point on it, he was lost.

This was not unusual. Cedric had got lost once (or maybe rather more than once) driving out of his own garage. And the fact of having no side windows, coupled with heavy and continuous rain which had turned his road map into blotting paper, more than adequately explains why he was thundering down an obscure side road 'somewhere in Somewhereland,' instead of cruising steadily down the A23 with a gaggle of other old smoky rattletraps.

Thundering is a word Willoughby used himself, and it is an apt one. His car's eight mighty cylinders, with bell-metal manifolds and folding baffles, combined to create the impression of the fires of Hell. The vehicle positively snorted. As the tailpipe poured forth alternate gushes of black smoke and brilliant flame, the four huge headlights glared whitely into the darkness and rain ahead. With the hoarse trumpeting of the fiercely-gunned engine, it was a machine to inspire terror and excitement.

What occurred next did so literally in a flash of lightning. The thunder that followed was mingled with the shriek of brakes, the braying of Willoughby's klaxon, and the howling of metal as the magnificent conveyance piled into a tree. Then the noise of the rain flooded over all; heavy, insistent. And

Willoughby stared through his plate-glass at the figure which lay crumpled on the road in the light of the two lamps still intact.

He pushed his goggles up on to his forehead and leapt out of the car. It seemed impossible that he could have struck the pedestrian, yet here indeed was an unconscious form. A bent form, in a heavy, old fashioned overcoat. A cloth cap, corduroy trousers, heavy rough boots with nails and steel studs, a white comforter around a thin and sinewed neck. Doubtless, Cedric thought, some poor retired son of toil.

That incorrigible Old Etonian, I may say, presented no such normal picture. His heavy goggles pushed high up above his rather bulbous nose, he was dressed in an all-enclosing ankle-length overcoat with no fewer than six shoulder capes. What's more, his outfit was topped off with a magnificent Donegal driver's cap, panelled and crown-buttoned, with the peak to the rear. In the early part of the twenty first century, he must have looked unique. Indeed, as he was to learn, in one respect he looked just like a ghost. For at that moment the recumbent figure opened his eyes and spoke.

'Thank God,' said the soaking old fellow. 'Thank God. I thought that you was him, come back to haunt me after all these years. Thank God.'

Willoughby, presented with an exhausted, possibly injured, accident victim, proceeded with caution and humanity.

'Well I'm not, old chap,' he replied jovially. 'Not at all. Name of Willoughby, solid as a rock, not a hint of the spirit about me.

'Which reminds me,' he went on. 'Got a drop of brandy in the car, if it's not been bust! Put you back on your feet in a trice. Have you skipping about like a two-year-old.'

By the time Willoughby returned, the old chap was sitting in the road rubbing his eyes. He took the cup without a word, had a good swig, and coughed mightily for a couple of minutes. Then he said quietly: 'Armstrong Hardcastle Mouton Special Eight. 1907, with the whirling poppets and them silly cams you could never get out of her. Daft, I always thought.'

Cedric was astonished.

'Good heavens above,' he said. 'How *did* you know? There can't be more than three of them left in the world! This is absolutely incredible!'

'Ah,' replied his new friend. 'May not be so many about now, but I've worked on a few and that's a fact. Stripped 'em down and put 'em back together again. Why, one time...'

He tailed off, while Willoughby waited impatiently. 'Yes?' he said, at last. The old fellow blinked up at him through the blinding rain. 'Used to know a chap – rich chap. He was exceptional fond of Armstrong Hardcastles for a time. Had quite a few of 'em, one way and another. I tell you, when I saw you in that flash of lightning it give me quite a turn. Well, a terrible bad turn, matter of fact, that's why I fell down like I did, in the road. He's been dead for years.'

He took the bottle absent-mindedly and sipped quietly, his faded old eyes cast down to the gravel of the narrow little road. Finally he looked up at Willoughby, and laughed shortly.

'I thought you must be him, come back from the grave, daft as that might sound. Just like him you looked, in that cap and goggles, with your big red nose and great fat cheeks puffed out, and your capes flying round your shoulders. And then the car. Nineteen Nought Seven. That was the year, God help us.'

Willoughby – who was a leading expert on vintage port – let the remark about his nose go by. In short, he was hooked.

'Now look here, old fellow,' he said. 'Perhaps we ought to get you to shelter. You may be hurt, or suffering from shock. Do you live far away? Or should I drive you to the nearest hospital, just to be on the safe side?'

'Hospital!' said the old one, sharply. 'Not likely you don't!' And he unexpectedly leapt to his feet.

'Anyway, sir,' he went on, poking Cedric none too gently in the ribs with the bottle, 'if that Armstrong Hardcastle's going anywhere tonight I'm a Dutchman. It's a laying-up job, that.'

Willoughby looked at the sadly bent vehicle in dismay.

'By Jingo,' he said. 'That *is* a mess and no mistake. Well well. What am I going to do? I don't even know exactly where I am. Is there a garage handy? I'm rather in your hands, I'm afraid.'

The ancient figure was deep in thought. At last he looked up, smiling.

'I tell you what,' he said. 'I'll do something for you. For old times sake, as it were, although I don't know you from Adam. If you don't mind roughing it, if you don't mind dossing down at my place for a while...well, my quarters are just on the other side of that hedge. And it'll be a treat to put your motor car to rights. I wouldn't let a modern garage wind my clock, sir. But I know them machines like the back of my hand. I've done the cuckoo-springs on that very model on a pitch black winter midnight with my belly full of beer, and one arm in a sling. It'll be a real treat.'

Willoughby was flabbergasted. But, like the rest of us, he was not one to look a gift horse in the mouth. What a golden opportunity! A mechanic one could trust. A man who, though old, was obviously fit, spry and dedicated. A man who had changed the cuckoo-springs on a Mouton Special Eight! It was heaven sent!

'Sir,' he cried. 'You are right. No second-year apprentice to a third-rate tin can factory shall touch that splendid machine – I accept! But one thing extra, if I may make so bold. Who exactly did you think it was when you saw me in the lightning flash? And why, if it is not an impertinent question, did it inspire so much fear in you?'

The old eyes regarded him intently for a few seconds. Then the artificial silk scarf vibrated as the scrawny neck stretched with laughter.

When it had stopped, he said quietly: 'I thought you was a landowner as used to live in these parts long ago. A fat, rich, jolly sort of fellow who didn't give a dang for no one, least of all the poor.'

He laughed again as Willoughby reddened. Then he added simply:

'Toad. That was his name. I thought that you was Toad.'

The next week, Willoughby later told me seriously, was the truly happiest in his life. By day the plump, rather refined man of letters, stripped to his cavalry twill bags and expensive cotton vest, acted the part of labourer to the oil-stained and horny-handed mechanic. By night he sat opposite his friend, and listened fascinated to the tale he told in his cramped but cosy living room. And when the old fellow had drained his last mug of ale and tapped out his last pipe of the evening, Willoughby would settle down to burn the midnight oil in his dark and poky bedroom. This part gave him perhaps the greatest pleasure of all. To record the facts that so astonished him.

Sadly, however, his new life's work, his guarantee of literary honour (and possibly, he told me modestly, the Booker and Pulitzer prizes) ended in tragedy, as already intimated. After six days Baxter Ferret had declared both the motor car and the story finished, but agreed that Willoughby could return with voice recorders and with cameras (and a change of underwear). He gave him detailed directions, a last glass of beer, and a friendly 'See you again, sir!'

Alas, not so. Willoughby spent his last three months searching, and his last three minutes extracting my promise to tidy up his manuscript, and see it delivered to a waiting world; that is, to 'complete' the saga. Personally, I felt the fact that his nurses allowed him to drink port right up until the end (latterly through a straw), had blinded him to this last reality: his chronicle, like himself, was finished.

So this is it, then. The story of Brotherhood Hall. I hope that Cedric's ghost, if he has one, will be forgiving enough not to haunt me for failing to carry out my promise to the letter. For I intend to write not another word, except to express the pious hope that everyone involved in these long-past events found at least a measure of peace before they found the grave.

Jan Needle

2014

FOOD AND DRINK THE WILD WOOD WAY!

BREWING IN A FERRET HOLE. DAISY'S TASTE EXPLOSION. A RECIPE.

Brewing beer in the first part of the 21st century is a lot different from brewing beer in Daisy Ferret's day. She had a copper 'kettle' certainly, although today stainless steel is more usual, but the rest of her equipment was just kitchen gear. And there were no handy brewing shops – all her bulky ingredients, like malt, grain and hops, would have had to be delivered, probably from a distant maltster. In modern brewing, timing and temperature are critical, and calibrated to the nth degree. Daisy would have burnt wood and faggots on an open grate, and kept her eye on the kitchen clock. A wooden spoon, or perhaps a metal ladle, was her implement of choice for disciplining her workforce. In most breweries today, this practice has virtually died out. Health and Safety.

Daughter Dolly's chap, however – the redoubtable stoat named Boddington – came from a place called Greenfield, outside the Wood itself – and when they married and moved to the North, they adopted the name of his home patch for their operations. Greenfield Brewery still exists, on the edge of the Lancashire Pennines, not far from Manchester and Oldham, and still brews delightful ales. It is on a larger scale than Daisy Ferret's, but is by no means enormous. That way the beers can be personal, pure, original. It is breweries like this that saved Britain's greatest asset from the clutches of the multi-nationals.

The modern Dolly and her husband are Tony and Mary Harratt, and their brewer is a man called Richard Thomas. Unlike Daisy, they produce up to three hundred and sixty gallons of beer every week, not just for their family and for thirsty passing neighbours. This 'reconstructed' recipe for

Daisy's Special makes a good and powerful bitter – five per cent alcohol by volume – and is reminiscent of another beer of theirs called Bill 'o Jack's, which commemorates a very famous murder only a mile from the brewery more than a hundred years ago. Daisy Ferret would have loved it!

Here are the ingredients. Unless you have a very large family, or circle of friends, the quantities will very likely need to be scaled down. The Greenfield Brewery 'liquor' (the technical name for the water that is the basis of the beer) comes straight off Saddleworth Moor, as a spring. A large part of the flavour of any beer is imparted by the liquor it is brewed from. This recipe will make a hundred and eighty gallons.

Malt:
Five sacks of Maris Otter
20 kgs of Crystal
15 kgs of wheat

Hops:
780 grams of WGV
300 grams of Tettnang

(Second addition):
600 grams of Fuggles
250 grams of Cascade

Copper fining tablets: 26
Start up specific gravity 1046

Method:

After it comes from the spring, the heated water (hot liquor) is maintained at 72 °C. The required quantity is transferred to the copper (or stainless steel) vessel called the mash tun.

The grist (dry mixture of malt and malted barley) is added to the liquor, where it sits for an hour, not unlike a thick porridge, while the sugar and colour is leached out of it. It is then transferred to another vessel called the kettle, where it is sparged (that is, the remaining sugars are washed from the grain).

The kettle is then brought up to the boil, when the first 'addition' of hops is made. After fifty minutes of boiling, the second addition of hops, plus the fining tablets, are introduced. The whole is then boiled for a further ten minutes.

In a modern brewery, a heat-exchanger would then bring the boiled fluid (the wort) down to 19/20 °C for transfer to the fermenting vessel. In Daisy's time, it would have been ladled into a stone trough, or vat, to cool it to a good room (or hole) temperature for the 'pitching' of the yeast. If fed and kept warm, yeast will live forever. Brewers have their own favourites, which they nurture like a pampered child, but you can buy it from a brewing shop.

Once pitched, the yeast will do what is has been up to since time began – 'eat' the sugar, and turn it into alcohol and carbon dioxide. Daisy's Special would probably have taken four or five days to produce 5 per cent alcohol by volume of beer (ABV). Brewday, her killer barley wine, would have been left fermenting for seven days or more.

Hers, like the lovely beers of Greenfield Brewery, continue to 'condition' (that is, stay alive to consume the remaining sugars) while in the bottle or the cask. As Mrs Ferret used to put it – lively beers for lively animals. And death to Mr Toad!

THE BANQUET AT BROTHERHOOD HALL

Although they did not survive in the main MS, some notes were recently discovered in a damp and grubby corner of the Ferret family burrow. They consist of what was possibly a speech, some jottings, and a recipe (or two?). They are included here for interest rather than enlightenment.

Brothers, (one page of them begins), there has been a slight falling out over the most suitable centrepiece of the proposed banquet to celebrate our triumph. Boddington Stoat proposed (and was seconded by Dolly Ferret, who in the opinion of her brother Baxter 'should have known better') a simple but nourishing meal of fish and chips, with salt ad lib and lashings of vinegar, maybe a pickled onion or two 'if the exchequer will stretch that far.' Other members of the committee objected strongly to this, especially Sherwood who, perhaps on account of his funny eye, once had an interesting encounter with a local crayfish and declared that any item of similar provenance would be served 'over his dead body.' Tetley (traction engine) thought that 'something steamed would hit the spot,' while others, in possibly a rather tasteless reference to Radcliffe Weasel, considered roly-poly pudding 'might be fun.'

Many of the younger elements mentioned pizza, or burger and fries, which the older Wooders claimed never to have heard of, on the grounds they had not been invented yet. Harrison the gunsmith wanted sausages and mash (although he'd settle for any item 'so long it was a banger'), and the kitchen staff plumped for anything that 'didn't need no washing up.' After hours of fruitless wrangling (on the grounds that 'some of us don't like fruit') it was agreed that the Chief Weasel should be the final arbiter.

'I suggest a simple dish,' he told the meeting, 'which is filling, nourishing, yet in a humble way extraordinarily opulent. For the outlay of not a large amount of cash it will feed an inordinate amount of inordinately hungry animals, and some greedy ones to boot. (I name no names, Radcliffe, but I'm sure you take my point). The bulk items are eggs, and milk, and flour, and the main ingredient is one that should not cost too much. In fact, we have already secured it.'

'Secured it?' said Dolly. 'But I do all the buying-in, OB, and I haven't been to Mr Wilson's for days. Secured what?'

'A toad,' said the Chief Weasel. 'And furthermore, your own dear mother Daisy has agreed to cook it for us. Her version of Mrs Beeton's most famous recipe.'

'A Toad?' said Boddington. 'Am you gone mad, Weasel? You want that we should eat that bloated plutocrat! Am you stark raving puddled?'

But now, the notes reveal, the other animals were laughing. For Daisy's toad was in no wise an edible amphibian but a sausage, in the hole. A clump of sausages indeed, good and spicy, blanketed in batter of the most crisp and succulent, and drowned in steaming gravy. It was a dish to relish and to cherish, and became an instant classic, both in the Wood and out of it. It is a fitting accompaniment, indeed, for the sort of ale that Daisy brewed, and in her turn her daughter Dolly, up in Greenfield.

Here is Ma's Toad. The spelling and sentiments are hers alone.

A body needs two sossies per ferret (three for greedier animals, half for a skinny stoat).

Two eggs per four ditto, depending likewise on the size and quantity.

112.4332 grams (approx) of flour (plain).

Portion of milk ad lib (to make a batter not too stiff, but needing to be stiffish).

Glass (similar in hold to that above) of Daisy's Special (poured by a mature lady; boychaps not trusted or trustworthy.)

Half a cupful of good beef dripping.

(All above to make enough for three, or so, depending on the season).

Method:

Fry the sossijeez till brown in half the dripping (metric).

Get a strong young animal (badger beats better batter) to beat batter till thick, beer makes better batter better (even).

Melt rest of the fat in tray in oven till sizzling and smoke is blue beware spontaneous combusschen. (Can get hot).

Batter over bottom of the tray. Sossies over bottom of the batter (Viz sleepy child in bed).

Close hoven door and cook for 'alf a hourish.

Dispose extraneous beer down throat.

Serve on best china plates with rest of fatty liquid over. Plus gravy. Plus peas. Smack lips to taste.

Alternative recipe (Young Saunders Ferret fecit): First catch your Toad. Batter him. Put him in a hole. Avoid Ma's wooden spoon; it hurts.

Books by Jan Needle

THRILLERS
Death Order
Other People's Blood
Kicking Off
The Bonus Boys

HISTORICAL NAVAL
A Fine Boy for Killing
The Devil's Luck
Nelson: The Poisoned River

SOCIAL REALISM
Killing Time at Catterick

CHILDREN AND YA
Silver and Blood – Return to Treasure Island
My Mate Shofiq
Albeson and the Germans

And many more

See also Annie Gauger's excellent The Annotated Wind in the Willows (W.W. Norton and Co.)

Bitter recipe supplied by Greenfield Brewery

www.hereforthebeer.co.uk/greenfield

Other Titles from Golden Duck

The Yachtsman Volunteers Collection:

- *The Cruise of Naromis: August in the Baltic 1939*
  GA Jones (with an introduction & afterword by Julia Jones)
- *Man the Ropes: the Autobiography of Augustine Courtauld—Explorer, Naval Officer, Yachtsman*
  Augustine Courtauld (with an introduction by Susie Hamilton)
- *From Pole to Pole: the Life of Quintin Riley*
  Jonathon Riley
  (with a foreword by Noël Riley)
- *Maid Matelot: Adventures of a Wren Stoker in World War Two*
  Rozelle Raynes (with a foreword by Hugh Matheson and an appreciation by Richard Woodman)
- *We Fought Them in Gunboats* (HMS *Beehive* edition)
  Robert Hichens
  (with a foreword by Tamsin Clive)

The Lionesses of the Sea Collection:

- *When I Put Out to Sea*
  Nicolette Milnes Walker (with an introduction by Katy Stickland and an afterword by the author)
- *The Seabird* (ebook, Summer 2023)
  Rozelle Raynes
- *The Tuesday Boys* (ebook, Summer 2023)
  Rozelle Raynes
- *North in a Nutshell*
  (ebook, forthcoming Summer 2023)
  Rozelle Raynes
- *My Ship is So Small*
  (ebook, forthcoming Summer 2023)
  Ann Davison

You may also be interested in *Uncommon Courage: The Yachtsman Volunteers of World War II* by Julia Jones, published by Adlard Coles, additionally available as an audiobook.

The East Coast:

- *The Deben* (biannual magazine)
  River Deben Association
- *Waldringfield: A Suffolk Village beside the River Deben*
  Waldringfield History Group

We also sell Robert Simper's books on East Coast history, people, and boats.

The Strong Winds Series by Julia Jones (with illustrations by Claudia Myatt):

1 *The Salt-Stained Book*
  (available as an audiobook)
2 *A Ravelled Flag*
3 *Ghosting Home*
4 *The Lion of Sole Bay*
5 *Black Waters*
6 *Pebble*
7 *Voyage North*

Books by Claudia Myatt:

- *Anglo-Saxon Inspirations: Designs to Colour and Create*
- *Keeping a Sketchbook Diary*
- *One Line at a Time: Why Drawing Is Good for You and How to Do It*
- *Sketchbook Sailor*
- *Antarctica: A Sketchbook*
  (forthcoming Summer 2023)

We hold most titles in Claudia Myatt's RYA *Go Sailing!* series.

For a full list of Golden Duck titles, including the Allingham family series, *Wild Wood* by Jan Needle and the *Please Tell Me* activity books for older people, see golden-duck.co.uk. Most are additionally available as ebooks.